MW01515612

The Hermit

Elizabeth H. Noble

RoseDog  Books

PITTSBURGH, PENNSYLVANIA 15222

ISBN # 0-8059-9257-X
Printed in the United States of America

First Printing

For information or to order additional books, please write:
RoseDog Books
701 Smithfield St.
Pittsburgh, PA 15222
U.S.A.
1-800-834-1803
Or visit our web site and
on-line bookstore at www..rosedogbookstore.com

Chapter One

He'd show them. They'd be sorry. Timmy biked down the sidewalk. Yeah, they'd be sorry when he was gone. Making him work all day, picking up his room and raking leaves and not letting him go play baseball. All that because he'd forgotten to wipe the dishes last night.

He watched a worm humping its way over the sidewalk. It looped over a twig and then Timmy carefully rode over it. He delighted in the squash. He felt bigger as he biked on.

It had been easy to slip away while his mother was talking over the back fence. She was always gabbing. She wouldn't even care he'd gone. Probably woudn't even notice. Just a slave—that's all he was.

Two squirrels chased each other circularly around a tree. He stopped to watch them, grinning in sympathy as they played. Grown ups didn't know how to enjoy life. All they thought of was work. Speeding along in the gentle sun of spring with the exhilaration of his manufactured wind blew out his anger. His legs pumped effortlessly and shortly he was on the outskirts of town. He would go up into the hills. He and his father had gone up there once, but his mother wouldn't let him go so far. She was such a scaredy cat.

The sun became warmer and he began pumping harder as the road started up a gentle rise, past an abandoned schoolhouse. He hardly noticed it. Who cared about schoolhouses but he rather wondered why it wasn't used any more. It didn't look that old.

He was big now. His mother didn't think so, insisting he have a baby sitter after school! He'd prove how big by going up the hill now. When they heard from him years later, after he had become a famous pirate, he would be rich and everybody would be afraid of him. They'd be sorry then that they had driven him out of the house.

The hill became steeper and he had to stand up to pump. Sweat gathered on his forehead. Panting, he looked up at the top of the hill, and muttered, "I can make it!" With fierce drives of each leg he forced the wheels to move forward. Chewing his tongue, he pushed the pedals down. He was barely moving. Then he glanced up. Only a little way more. With a tremendous surge of power he kept the bike moving to the crest of the hill. He'd done it!

"Ki-yi," he yipped as the downgrade took over and he coasted faster and faster. Laughter bubbled out. He lifted his face to the speeding wind and gripped the handle bars tightly as he raced down the slope. Momentum took him half way up the next hill. Before the coasting stopped, he was frantically pedaling. He could do it. He'd done it before.

2

The Hermit

But this hill was higher and forced him to put his feet down to keep the bike upright. He looked back. His town was small with green trees screening houses so they were just spots of white. Well, it was the last time he'd see it. He was on his own now.

Slogging forward, pushing his bike, he caught a glimpse of something. It was a wild cat. He stopped. The big tawny animal lifted its head and he saw a black and wrinkled forehead. Not a wild cat. It was a dog. Sure a big one. He hesitated. His mother always said he shouldn't pat strange dogs. Besides, this was a pretty big one. The dog stood staring at him.

"Hi," Timmy said uneasily.

The dog's tail moved slightly.

"What's your name?"

Another movement caught Timmy's eye. An old woman came out of the bushes. The dog bayed. Timmy stepped backward.

The woman looked up and said to the dog, "'S all right." She was picking blackberries and paying no attention to Timmy.

He moved forward, pushing his bike. "Is that your dog?"

"No."

"He's sure a big one."

No answer. "Would he mind if I pet him?"

She shrugged.

"What's his name?"

"Dog."

"That's not a name!" But he turned to the dog. "Dog, may I pat you?" He dropped his bike in the ditch and went toward the animal.

The face smiled, the tail wagged. Timmy approached, his hand out. The dog did not

3

move. As Timmy reached out to him, the dog made interrogatory sniffs.

Timmy's hands could not spread aross the big head. He fluffed the lop ears. "He's nice. Whose dog is he?"

"His."

"Whose?" Timmy looked at the woman in her beltless brown dress. She wore a tattered straw hat with part of a tired rose on it.

She continued picking berries.

"Are those berries good to eat?"

"'Course."

Timmy reached out and picked some, cramming them into his mouth. Their warmed sweetness was good. "Where do you live?"

There was no answer, no pause in her picking.

"Does Dog live there too? My grandfather had a dog once. He said it wasn't his—just came and lived with him."

No reply.

"What kind of dog is he?"

"Good."

"I mean what kind—a German Shepherd? He's not that, I know. Is he a Saint Bernard?"

She strained to reach higher branches and did not answer.

"Do you want me to help?" Timmy started picking berries from the lower branches and tossing them into her basket. "I live down there," he offered, pointing to the distant town. No answer.

As Timmy picked, he stumbled over a big stick. He picked it up and threw it away. The dog plummeted after it, brought it back and Timmy grabbed it. They tussled until bark caught in the dog's throat. He retched it up.

The Hermit

Timmy threw the stick again, but it was ignored.

"What are you going to do with these berries?"

"Eat."

"Do you make jam? My mother used to before she went to work. She doesn't have time any more." His interest flagged and he dropped down beside the dog, fondling the ears. "His ears are so soft."

Without a word, the woman started down the road. Dog rose, pushing Timmy over, and followed her. Timmy ran over, picked up his bike and rode slowly alongside the woman. The dog ranged in the field, checking back on them every so often.

"You live up here? I didn't know anybody lived up here." She trudged along, silent.

He stole a look at her long, straight nose jutting out over the protruding chin. She looks like a witch, he thought and heard himself asking, "Are you a witch?'

Her laugh cackled.

"Did I make you mad? I didn't mean to."

No answer.

"You don't talk much." She abruptly turned up a faint path. He tried to ride the bike but the grass made it hard. Getting down, he walked beside her.

"I'm running away." He glanced sideways expecting the usual grown up's response. No reaction.

"Did you run away?" he asked "Is that why you're here?"

She glared at him. "Go home."

He stared. "Why?"

"Go home!" she ordered and swung her arm at him. He backed up a few steps.

"What did I do?"

"Go home!" She reached down and pulled up a stick and brandished it at him.

Avoiding the stick, Timmy stumbled over his bike and fell backwards. she walked on. Timmy slowly got up, turned his bike and plowed through the grass, heading home.

Chapter Two

The old woman's chasing him away was a barb in Timmy's mind. What had he done that made her so mad? He wanted to go back, and that didn't make sense. It's the dog, he thought. But it wasn't entirely. He kept thinking of the old woman. She was so different. No one he knew lived all alone. People were always clustering.

However, it was some time later that Timmy sneaked away from the baby sitter and biked up to the place where he'd seen the old woman and the dog. He stopped and looked around. No woman. No dog. He thought briefly of picking some berries and taking them to her—except he didn't know where to take them. Besides, he didn't have anything to carry them in.

Guess I climbed the hill for nothing, he thought. And then a movement caught his eye. It was a tawny flash. The dog! He waited and watched. The dog raced down the field and then pounced. What was he doing?

Timmy abandoned his bike and pushed his way through the weeds. The dog was a lump in the grass. As Timmy got close he saw the dog tearing at something he held in his paws. The head rose and a growl told Timmy to keep his distance.

Timmy looked closely, then exclaimed, "You bad dog. You've got a rabbit!" Dog continued to eat and Timmy realized that the old woman was not buying food for the dog, he was on his own. Timmy sat down until the meal was over and waited. The dog rose lazily and started off.

"Dog! Wait for me." Dog turned his head, hesitated and then went on. Timmy ran after him, calling, "Are you taking me to the old woman?" It was not easy running in the long grass and Timmy fell. Dog came back and regarded him intently.

"Hi, Dog. Where's your owner?"

Dog's tail swished and he came closer. There was a little blood on his muzzle beyond the sweep of his tongue. He put his head down and Timmy patted it. "You taking me to your home?" Timmy rose and stroked the dog. Dog leaned against him.

"C'mon, I'll take you home—'cept you're going to have to show me where it is." The two of them set out.

Dog was in no hurry, sniffing the earth, tall weeds.

"Are you taking me home or are we just walking?" Timmy asked. But shortly thereafter he saw the slight path he and the woman had taken before she'd sent him home. Now all he had to do was follow the path and it would surely lead him to the old woman.

But it was some time before he saw the falling down house. The roof was sway backed like a hard-used horse. Some glass glinted in the sun, but most of the windows were gone. The frame of a screen door, minus the screen, dangled on one hinge. The house was black with assaults of the weather. Timmy would have passed it, but the dog was bounding toward it. This was where the old woman lived?

Timmy followed the dog, suddenly wondering why he'd come.

Dog rushed over to a lump on the ground and The old woman reared up, gave the dog a tug on its ears and went back to her digging.

"Hi. Your dog brought me."

Fierce eyes repelled him. "Wha'cha doing here?"

"Just visiting. Do you want me to help pull out the weeds?" He squatted and started tugging at the weeds.

"Picking."

"Picking?" He looked at the gnarled dirt encrusted hands plucking leaves quickly. "Why?"

"Eat."

"You eat weeds!"

"God provides."

"Nobody eats weeds!"

Dog flopped by the old woman. Timmy broke the silence. "Do you cook them or eat them raw?"

"Both"

Her hand dropped leaves into an old apron spread beside her. She leaned closer and took out a few, discarding them.

Timmy retrieved a leaf and asked, "This is a big one. Why don't you want it?"

"Tough."

"Oh." He dropped to his knees and started picking leaves but when he went to dump them in the apron, she stuck out her thin, boney arm.

"No." She pointed to a tuft of weeds. "Those."

"You want those? My father's always digging them out. He hates them. Calls them sore fingers."

The woman was busy picking. Timmy did the same, carefully choosing the smaller leaves. He showed them to the woman, "Are these o.k.?" She nodded. He picked in silence, asking her approval before he dumped the weeds in the apron.

"You live here?" No answer so he persisted, "All alone?"

"Me and Dog."

"Why do you just call him 'Dog'? That's not a fun name."

No answer. He continued, "Aren't you ever scared?" As usual there was no answer. "I tried camping out once in my back yard. I got scared." No response. He surveyed the house. At the front he could now see a sagging porch. "It's not a very good house." Thinking that sounded rude, he added quickly, "It has a nice view, though."

The woman gathered up her apron of weeds, heading for the house. Timmy followed. Had he made her mad? They went in through the flopping screenless door. It was dim in here, but Timothy saw a charcoal burner with a pot of water, boiling, on it. She dumped the leaves into it and set a square of wood on it as a lid.

"You didn't wash them" he exclaimed in horror. Then he noticed she didn't have a sink. What a peculiar house. There was a table, and drawn up to it was a big wooden box. He realized she was cooking her meal and it wasn't much. He stuck out his hand. "Good bye. I'm sorry, I don't know your name."

She turned away and went to an upended box and took out a chipped plate. Timmy went to the door, heard something and stopped. He looked back. She was scrabbling in a box, there was a metallic clink and she came up with a big metal slotted spoon. He waited, thinking she had spoken. She did not look at him.

I guess I imagined it. I was sure she'd said, 'Come again.'

She handed Timmy a piece of brown bread and held out a pan of stewed fruit. He lookd for a knife to spread the fruit on his bread. Saying nothing, she took his bread and dipped it into the berry sauce.

He bit into the bread. The sauce was tart, black berries, but they tasted good. The bread was bitter.

He looked surprised. "What kind of bread is this?"

"Acorn."

"Acorn! Nobody eats acorns!"

"Indians. Important."

Secretly he fed his bread to the dog. The dog must be an Indian—he liked it. "Don't you ever go to the store?"

"No."

"Why?"

She did not answer, dipped her own bread into the berry sauce and then said, "No money."

"None at all?" Everybody had money!

She shrugged.

"How do you manage?"

She swept her arm in a circle. "God gives."

Timmy looked at her in awe. Why they were always going to the store. How did one get along without money?

They sat there for awhile in silence. Dog had stretched out beside Timmy.

Suddenly the old woman said, pointing to the houses visible in the valley below. "Fraid."

"They're afraid? Naw, I live down there. We're not afraid."

"Huddle," she said. "No sun, no stars, no rain. Poor things."

He stared at her. "You feel sorry for us? Gee, we have good things, white bread 'n bologna and TV 'n computers and cars. Don't you wish you had a car?"

"Got sky. You look?"

"At the sky? Sure, sometimes. It's pretty today."

"Night?"

"I'm sorta scared of the dark."

She nodded. "People scared. Own things."

"But you have to work so hard to get things to eat—picking weeds and berries and stuff."

"Free."

"I'm not sure I'd want to be that free."

They sat quietly for awhile. He asked, "What about winter? Don't you get cold?"

She nodded but added, "Sun good."

"I could bring you some blankets. Mom has lots!"

"No!" Her black eyes blazed at him.

"Why not?" She was towering over him,

blasting at him, "No! No!" as she had that first day.

"Don't tell."

"I haven't. I won't."

In answer to her glare he got up and said, "I have to go home now."

She continued to glare at him and he left.

Were they all afraid? Yes, kinda. Mom was always worrying about him, telling him not to talk to anyone. And news was always about somebody getting killed. He thought of his house and realized it was comfortable, even pretty compared to some of his friends' houses. Were they in it because they were afraid He'd have to ask his father tonight. When he biked into his driveway, he noted that they had a security company notice in the window. He'd always known it but he hadn't thought. He wouldn't have to ask his father. He knew. They were afraid.

Chapter Three

His mother was home and Timmy was trying to slip out the back door. She caught him.

"Where are you going?"

"Just out."

"Out where? Mrs. Richards has told me you're disappearing for hours. What are you doing?"

"Riding my bike and seeing a friend."

"What friend?"

Timmy hesitated. Should he say 'Dog'? He didn't think his mother would approve of it if he said an old woman, and besides, he did-n't know her name. "I don't know his name."

"You've been playing with him for some time, apparently."

"Not very long."

"Where does he live?"

"Up Sycamore Drive."

"That's a long way."

"Why I ride my bike."

"How did you meet him?"

"He has a dog. It got away."

"How come you don't know his name?"

"Didn't ask."

"I don't think you can go. Why don't you call him and ask him to come down here?"

"Can't. Don't know his name."

His mother looked at him and then suggested, "Suppose we go to the zoo."

"I promised him I'd come. You said never to break a promise."

"I don't like it when you play with people I don't know. Can't you do something with Brian Thomas?"

"He's at his grandmother's."

"O. K., stay home. You may not go out."

"Why?"

"Because I don't know whom you're playing with. How about playing Russian Bank with me?"

"No, you always win."

"It's a card game. It's luck."

"You're telling me to break a promise?"

"Timmy, for a change I'm home today. Let's make the most of it."

"But he's my friend." His voice rose in a whine.

"And I'm not?"

Timmy's shoe scraped a circle. "You're my mother."

"Well, heaven forbid you have to spend some time with your mother!"

"But she's lonely. She's all alone."

"I thought you said this was a little boy."

"Is, partly."

"How can it be partly?"

"The dog's a boy."

"But it's the little girl you want to see."

"Mostly the dog."

"Great. You prefer a dog to your mother."

The Hermit

"Not all the time. Just today, 'Cause I promised."

"Promised the dog?"

"Well, yeah. But her too."

"This sounds fishy to me. You're not going." She turned away and then turned back. "Suppose we both go."

"No!" Timmy panicked.

"So you're ashamed. How'd you meet her?"

"I told you. The dog was lost,."

His mother turned away. "You're not leaving this house today."

"Aw, gee."

He watched as she went to her desk. He thought of diving out the door, but by the time he'd brought his bike around, she'd be after him. He went over and picked up a car hiding by the sofa.

His mother said, "It's not a bad idea. Suppose I drive you there—just so I can meet this girl and dog."

"Too late now."

"Cutting off your nose to spite your face?" And then she turned to him sharply, "Or you don't want me to meet her?"

Timmy ignored his mother, pulling down some books to make a tunnel for his car. He could get away from Mrs. Richards easily. He pushed his car through the tunnel and knew without looking that his mother was watching him, a frown creasing between the lenses of her glasses.

Chapter Four

It had not been easy to fool Mrs. Richards.
Apparently his mother had warned her not to
let Timmy out of her sight. She kept checking on him. His chance came when she'd gotten a long call from her daughter. Timmy managed to slip out the front door, race around
to the garage and grab his bike and pedal off.
It was important he go. This was the end of
July and school would be starting and then he
couldn't go.

The hill seemed harder now since he hadn't
been up it in several weeks. No one was in
the field when he rode down. No matter. He
pedalled to the path and started down it. It
was a long way and it was hard to bike through
the grass even if it was trampled down. No
one had appeared and he was up to her house.

He called, "Dog, Dog." There was no answer.
Was she gone? She had been so afraid that he
would tell, maybe she had moved on. He felt
guilty as he pushed the door open and went
in.

There was a low growl. Step by reluctant

step, Timmy proceeded. Hesitantly he glanced into the bedroom and saw the dog on the bed. "Dog?" he asked as he went closer. The growl was more pronounced. Surprised, Timmy stared. He'd growled at him before when he had the rabbit and meant it. "What's the matter, Dog?"

Cautiously the boy advanced and then realized the dog was lying on the old woman. Her breathing was rough and rasping. He tried to think. He didn't know her name, he'd never addressed her by anything. Finally he managed, "Lady? Are you all right?"

Embarrassed, Timmy moved closer. The dog rose, straddling the body, his head was lowered as he growled.

"It's all right, Dog, I won't hurt her. I won't even touch her." Loudly he said, "Lady, I'm Timmy. Can I help you?"

No answer, just the heavy breathing that frightened him. "She's sick. I think I'd better get help."

He knew he should do something, but he had no idea what. He decided the only thing he could do was to go home and call 911. "I'm getting help for her, Dog."

Peddling his bike furiously, he ascended the hill with no trouble and then glided down. It was only a fast pedal home.

He ran into the house and to the phone and dialed 911. The operator answered and he babbled, "I need help. Someone's sick."

"What's your name? And your address?" Timmy gulped. What was the address?

"Little boy, do you know your address?"

"Two eleven Regal Street,"

"Who is sick? Your mother?"

The Hermit

"No." he couldn't even give a name.

"Who is sick? Someone in your family?"

"No."

The calm voice edged with anger. "This is not a joke. Calling 911 . . ."

"It isn't a joke! It's an old lady. She lives alone and she sounds terrible. I know where she lives, but not the address—not her name."

"You said she was at 211 Regal Street."

"That's my address. She's up Sycamore Hill Drive and then off that—I know where she is. I was just there."

"If this is a practical joke. . ."

"No, it isn't! Please come. Come to my house and I'll show you where she lives."

"What's your telephone number?"

"676-9211."

"Hang up. I'll call you back."

"Will you come?"

"Hang up."

"She needs help."

"Hang up."

Reluctantly he hung up. What could he do now? Mrs. Richards appeared.

"You! Where have you been? Your mother said I was to keep track of you and you just dis-appear."

"I went to see my friend and she's real sick and I tried to call 911 and they won't help."

The phone rang. Mrs. Richards grabbed it, glaring at the boy. In answer to her "Yes" came the message, "This is Emergency Services. Did someone just call 911?"

Mrs. Richards looked at Timmy. He nodded, "I called."

"Yes," she said, "a young boy just called."

"Whom is he calling about?"

Mrs. Richards turned, "What were you calling about?"

"An old lady. She's awfully sick"

Mrs. Richards relayed the message. She turned to Timmy, "Her address?"

"I don't know—and I don't know her name."

"Then how can they help?"

"Have them come here and I'll show them. Please hurry. She's real bad sick."

His baby sitter was talking into the phone. "Yes, this is 211 Regal Street. It's Mr. and Mrs. Thomas Hastings' home. It's their son that talked to you. He says he doesn't know the woman's name nor address but if you came he could show you." After a moment she turned to Timmy. "Describe how she's sick."

For a moment Timmy remained silent, "She's in bed, and didn't answer when I spoke to her. And she sounds terrible—her breathing, loud and raspy."

This information was relayed and then after Mrs. Richards listened, answered, "Yes, I do think he's sincere. He is very upset." Again she listened and answered, "He's been going off on his bike this summer and no one knew where . . . Thank you." She hung up. She turned to the boy. "They're sending an ambulance out here."

"Oh, thank you, Mrs. Richards. They just wouldn't believe me."

"They thought you were pulling a practical joke."

"Nobody believes kids."

"Who is this person?"

"She lives way out in a tumble down house

The Hermit

with a dog. She eats weeds and stuff. And she has this dog. He won't let you near her now. I don't know what they'll do about him."

"Maybe we'd better call the police."

"Oh, no! He's just protecting her."

"How about the Humane Society?"

"What would they do?"

"Maybe tranquilize the dog so they could help the woman."

Timmy hesitated. "They wouldn't believe me either. We'd have to wait again. Maybe Dog will let me get close. He knows me."

"What kind of dog is it? Is it big?"

Timmy shaded the truth. "Sort of middle size."

They heard a vehicle and Timmy ran to the door. It was the ambulance. He ran out and the driver let him jump in.

"O.k., kid, where's this no-name—no-address person?"

"I know where she lives. Go up Sycamore Drive—over the hill and down." The trip up and over the hill was so easy Timmy had a hard time relating it to his bike rides.

"Then there's a path—up there, just past that tree." He watched until he saw the slight indication, "There, up there."

"God, you expect me to drive up there!"

It's where her house is."

"Well, we'll try it. Is it far?" Cautiously the truck crept along. "Am I going to be able to turn around?"

"Yeah, I think so. Wait—there it is!" Cars went so much faster than feet.

"Somebody lives there?"

The ambulance stopped and Timmy leaped out and ran into the house. "Dog," he called. A

23

growl answered him. He went into the bedroom and stopped at the door. "It's all right, Dog. I've got help for her." The two paramedics came in behind him and the dog rose to his feet and roared.

"My god!"

"What is it?" The men were backing away.

Timmy hissed. "Go out. I'll try to get him calmed down." He turned to the dog. "It's all right. We've come to help. You know I won't hurt her. We're friends." Timmy was advancing a step at a time. "It's o.k., Dog." The tail was waving slightly. In front of the dog, the boy said, "Come on, Dog." Dog laid back down.

"You have to let the men come in." Slowly Timmy put out his hand toward the animal. "It's o.k. No one's going to hurt her. We're here to help."

Dog suffered Timmy's patting his head. "Get down, Dog."

Dog did not move. He had no collar. Timmy looked around to see if he could find something. Maybe the blanket. No that was too bulky. Then he remembered she had a clothesline. He ran outside and saw the two paramedics. He rushed to the pieced together clothesline and tried to untie it, but it was above his head. Would it hold Dog? One of the paramedics came over and untied the line.

"You gonna tie up the dog?"

"If I can get him to leave her." Timmy ran back in and walked up to Dog. "I'm sorry to do this, but we gotta do it if we're going to help her."

He stood there, patting the dog and then he slipped the rope around its neck and tied it with two knots. "Come on, Dog. Your job's

The Hermit

done." He took hold of the collar and the dog growled softly. "I know it's not fair. You're a good dog, but we have to let the men in." Suddenly the Dog jumped off the bed.

"Good boy!" Timmy led him to the porch and down the steps toward the lake, found a stout tree and tied the dog who immediately leaped and strained to get free. Timmy called to the paramedics, "Go get her. I'll try to keep him here." The dog's agonized efforts toppled Timmy. He grabbed the line of the plunging dog and scrambled to his feet. "It's all right, Dog. Take it easy. We're just trying to help." He attempted to soothe Dog and was glad to see the men finally come out with the stretcher. They were loading it into the ambulance, Dog struggling furiously. With a snap, the rope broke and Dog flew toward the ambulance. The driver jumped into the ambulance just as the dog hurled himself against the door. The driver yelled, "Hurry up, boy."

"What about Dog?"

"Leave him!"

"I'll walk back with him."

"That's about five miles!"

"I can walk that." The ambulance took off, Dog leaping after it. He threw himself against the back door and tumbled down into the road. He chased the ambulance out to the road but there the ambulance picked up speed and left him. Dog sat down and howled. Timmy caught up with him and threw his arms around him. "It's going to be all right. You can stay with me until she's well." He picked up the frayed end of the rope. "Come on, Dog," and they started walking.

Chapter Five

Shortly after they came home, his mother and father faced Tim. "What is all this about calling 911?" his father asked.

"I had to. She was terribly sick."

"Who is she?"

"I don't know her name. She's my friend."

"This is the same friend you were telling me about—the she-he-it friend?" His mother's voice was sharp and disbelieving.

"You wouldn't have liked her."

"Why not?"

"She was old and ate funny and lived without money. She said you were all afraid."

"You're damned right, I wouldn't have liked her. Why was she messing with you? What were you doing there?"

"We talked. I just liked her. And the dog."

"That elephant in our garage?" his father asked.

"Yeah, I guess."

"Let's get back to this woman. Where'd you meet her? And why?" His mother's eyes bored into him.

"I was out riding one day and saw the dog. Then I helped her pick some berries and then she sent me home."

"I take it you went back."

"Yeah. I wanted to see the dog again."

"And then what happened?"

"Nothin'." His mother's eyes commanded him to add something. "She was picking weed leaves—I helped."

"And what was she doing with these weed leaves?"

"Eating, I think. She was cooking them."

"And didn't that strike you as weird?"

"Yeah, but she didn't have anything else."

"A hippie," his father interjected. "I don't like it," his mother moved away reflectively. "What would an old woman want with a little boy? It bothers me."

"She was old?" his father asked.

"She had grey hair—I never asked how old she was."

"You didn't even ask her name!" his mother exploded. Timmy sat there, skewered by their angry eyes. "You know, the hospital may try to stick us for the bill. And we don't even know her name." This was from his father.

"How come you found out she was sick?"

"I just went up there, and she was in bed. Dog was on top of her, wouldn't let me come close."

"But you did. You got the dog off so the paramedics could get in. What were you thinking of?"

"I had to. She was sick and needed help."

They were silent, regarding him. His mother finally said, "I don't know whether I should praise you or scold you. You shouldn't

The Hermit

have run away there when you knew I didn't want you to go, but then again, you used your head and got help."

"Of course, you're going to be responsible for the hospital bill. Tough on a $3.00 a week allowance." His father laughed.

The subject was dropped, but Timmy knew he had to go to the hospital to see about his friend. A day later, Mrs. Richards occupied with television and his parents at work, Timmy rode his bicycle into town. It was not hard to find the hospital; what was scarey was ducking the cars. But he arrived and propped his bike against a railing and went in. He had been there with his parents when they visited his grandmother. It took only a moment for him to orient himself and go up to the information desk.

"There was an old woman brought here Friday. I don't know her name—you probably don't either. What room is she in?"

"Hard to find somebody without a name." The woman smiled at him but clicked her machine. "Probably this one—Jane Doe.

"She's—are you here by yourself? We don't allow children under fourteen upstairs with-out an adult with them."

"My mom's parking the car. She told me to come in and get the room number to save time."

Doubtfully she regarded him. "I think we'd better wait for your mother."

A burly man plowed up to the desk loudly demanding, "Amelia Cartwright's room. We're in a hurry."

The woman said aside to Timmy, "Tell your mother it's 1033." She turned to the man and hastily scanned the C's in the list.

Timmy scuttled to the elevators and got on with adults. The elevator was slow but eventually it arrived at the tenth floor. He slipped out and stared around. He didn't want to ask at the desk. He looked around at the doors and numbers.

"Little boy, what are you doing here?"

"I'm looking for my friend. Brought in Friday."

"We don't allow unaccompanied children up here. How did you get in.?"

"I just came."

"Well, suppose you just leave."

"Can you tell me how she is?"

"Is this your relative?"

"Not exactly."

The nurse laughed. "And what is she then— exactly."

"She's not my grandmother, but: she acts like it."

"Her name?"

"I'm not sure."

The nurse looked severe. "I don't know what you're trying to pull, but I think you'd better leave the floor." She ushered him to the elevator. "Don't come back."

How could he find out about her when he didn't know her name? Outside he sank down on the steps of the hospital. He needed to go in and see her.

A man came up and stopped. "What's the matter, kid? Mom in the hospital?"

"No."

"Just resting like a pigeon, huh?" The man looked around and noticed the bike. "Your bike?"

Timmy nodded.

The Hermit

The man settled on the step beside him. "Well, I don't think you rode your bike here just to sit. What's the story?"

Timothy gave him an appraising glance. "I have a friend in here, but I don't know her name."

"That's unusual. How come you don't know your friend's name? Just meet her?"

"She never told me. But she's real sick and I've got to see her."

"Are you sure she's in the hospital?"

The boy nodded. "Yeah, I saw the ambulance pick her up. I'd taken them to her house."

"Sounds like a story. But you don't know her name. She a neighbor?"

"No—lived alone way out in the country. She was different."

"Different? How?"

"She ate weeds and berries and stuff. She said she didn't have any money. She lived there with Dog."

"I came here, hoping to find a story. I think I may have one. Let's go in and see if we can find your friend."

"Her room is 1033," Timmy said rising happily.

"You know her room number? Why can't you go in?"

"They won't let me by myself 'cause I'm a kid."

"Problem solved." He put a hand on Timmy's shoulder and they marched in together. Up on the tenth floor, the man, with Timmy, whispered "When did you say she came in?"

"Friday. It was in the afternoon."

The man addressed a nurse. "You have a Jane Doe here who came in Friday afternoon—brought by ambulance. Can we see her?"

"She's not supposed to have visitors."

"My little friend here. . ."

"You're the one who was in here earlier. Didn't I tell you not to come back?"

"He's with me," the reporter interfered, his hand firmly on Timmy's shoulder. "What's wrong with her?"

"She had a stroke."

"But she's not in intensive care."

"No hospitalization. Who's going to pay for it?"

"We'd like to see her."

"I told you. No visitors."

"Why?"

The nurse struggled with this a minute and then shrugged. "Just for a minute." She led them to 1033 and they entered.

Timmy hardly reognized the clean, pale faced woman, her hair neatly brushed back. Her breathing was still noisy and harsh. He touched her hand.

"She's still sick." He looked at the tubes and plastic bags by her bed. "It scares me."

"She's being taken care of. Let's go downstairs." In the elevator the man got Timmy's name and address and bade him goodbye at the curb. He had his story.

Chapter Six

It was the next night at supper that a knock came at the Hastings' home. Mrs. Hastings answered the door.

"Mrs. Hastings? I'm Robert Kendall, from THE BUGLE. I met your son yesterday down at the hospital, and he took me up to see his friend. As I understand it, he called 911 and got the paramedics to go up there and get her. A brave and resourceful kid. Could I come in and talk to you people about him? We'd like to run an article about this."

"Well, I don't know. . ."

"The article, I assure you, will be in his favor. There are just a few things we'd like to clear up."

Intrigued, Timmy's mother hesitated, and the reporter stepped inside. "I really do thank you for your time."

Defeated, she waved toward the dining room. "We're just finishing dinner. Would you have a cup of coffee?"

"That would be nice." He entered the room and went to Timmy's father. "Mr. Hastings?

I'm Bob Kendall from THE BUGLE. I talked with your son yesterday and would like more information on his story."

Mr. Hastings glanced angrily at his wife. "I don't think we have anything to say."

"Oh, I'm sure you do. Your son is a remarkable boy, as I'm sure you're aware—a chip off the old block, probably."

Kendall sat down and grinned over at Timmy. "We really want to do some stories about kids doing good instead of bad. How did you feel about his friendship with this old lady?"

Mrs. Hastings cut off her husband's remark, "We really didn't know much. We knew Timmy was sneaking away from his baby sitter—I work—but he was always home for supper. I did find out about it, a little before he found her sick, but he didn't tell me much."

Timmy who had been listening, dropped his head.

"I don't think we want anything published, young man, and I'd appreciate it if you'd leave." Mr. Hastings rose to his full, arresting height.

"We do want you to give us your side, Mr. Hastings," Kendall said, still seated. "If this was a surprise to you, it must have been disturbing."

"It is," Mrs. Hastings said. "I can't help wondering why this woman snared my son."

"She didn't trap me," Timmy interjected. "She didn't want me there at first. But I think she was lonely."

"How long had she been up there?" Kendall quickly asked. Mr. Hastings was slowly subsiding into his chair.

"I don't know. She had some things. She had

a bed, she had a charcoal burner, she burned wood. She didn't have a sink—I think she used the lake. It had a pretty view."

"Do you think you could take me there some-time?" Kendall asked.

"Sure. Now?"

The reporter glanced at the parents. Mrs. Hastings protested, "It's getting late."

"We'd have time," Timmy said and glanced at the reporter, "You do have a car don't you?" At the answering nod, he said, "It's not so far by car as it is by bicycle."

The reporter laughed. "I bet it isn't. Mr. Hastings, did you want to go with us?"

The answer was a curt nod. The three of them rose, Timmy rushing to the door. They went out to the reporter's 1980 Plymouth and got in, Timmy taking the front passenger seat.

"I'll show you how to get there. You go up Sycamore Drive."

As the car struggled up the slope, Kendall observed, "This must have been a b—some hill to climb on your bike."

Timmy nodded. "It was, but I always made it. Keep on going down." Back on the flat, he glued his eyes to the window.

"You really have to watch now. There's a path—there it is." He turned to his father. "We should have brought Dog."

His father's dissenting grunt was the only answer.

"We'd better walk from here. The ambulance made it, but your car might not."

Timmy jumped out and ran a little ahead and then turned around to face them as he walked backward. "The first time I saw her, she was back there picking berries." He waved his arm back the way they had come. "It was Dog I saw first." He laughed at himself, "I thought he was a wild cat at first."

"A wild cat?"

"He was brown and big. Of course when I saw his face, I knew it was a dog."

"I believe it's a bull mastiff, an expensive dog. She must have stolen it." Mr. Hastings interjected.

"She didn't steal it!"

"How did she get it?" Kendall asked.

Timmy shrugged his shoulders. "I don't know."

"Then you don't know she didn't steal it."

"She didn't steal. She lived here just using weeds and stuff."

His father humphed. He was getting breathless from the difficult walking.

"How did she get here?"

"I don't know," Timmy answered the reporter. "She didn't talk much."

They came within sight of the house. The reporter whistled. "How could she live there?"

"She lived there in winter, too," Timmy said proudly. "She said the sun felt good."

They went toward the derelict place. The reporter went in first, then Timmy. Mr. Hastings followd reluctantly.

"She didn't have much," the reporter said. He went into the bedroom and looked at the bed and under it. "It has cinder blocks holding up one side." He examined the charcoal burner and saw that it was also propped up on one side. "Think she scrounged everything from a dump."

36

The Hermit

Mr. Hastings scrunched inside himself as if he would be contaminated by the dirt in the house. Timmy went out on the sloping porch. "See, you can see our town. She said we were all afraid."

"Afraid of what?" the reporter asked, his words tangled with Timmy father's, "Get in here before that porch collapses."

Timmy ignored his father. He answered the reporter. "She said nobody enjoyed the sun or the stars or the moon." He added confidentially, "Living in houses showed they were afraid."

Mr. Hastings called, "Come on, Timmy. We've got to leave." He left the house, muttering, "A crackpot."

"Was she hiding here?" Kendall asked.

Timmy started to shake his head and then decided against it. "Maybe. She told me not to tell my mother." And then he said in surprise, "She was afraid!"

"Afraid of being found, anyway. Tell me, Timmy, did she have any boxes to keep papers in?"

Timmy pointed to the upended box that held her chipped dish and a glass. "That's all I ever saw. She kept some cooking things there."

Kendall went over and reached in and found a newspaper. He pulled it out. It was dated three years before. He folded it up and put it back. "I think your father is anxious to leave. Let's go. She was a brave and resourceful woman, Timmy."

Timmy glanced at him. That was the same thing he'd said about him. Did he say it about everybody? But he said nothing. "She ate things that grow wild, you know. She knew what she could eat—once I gave her some leaves and she threw them away. She was smart."

"She must have been to have survived out here all this time. By the way, I called the hospital. She's regained consciousness." He glanced at the boy. "She's paralyzed on her left side. You did know she had a stoke?"

"The paramedics said that, I think. What's going to happen to her?"

"She'll probably be sent to the charity ward in Dublin's hospital."

Timmy stopped and scraped the dirt around a weed with his foot. "She won't like that."

"I'm going to try to find some of her family."

"Maybe we could take her," Timmy offered.

The reporter glanced up at Timmy's father striding away. "I wouldn't count on it."

Chapter Seven

Timmy was back in school and the days were getting shorter. He had not been back to the hospital to check on his friend. One evening he was surprised when his mother called him to the phone. "For you," she said, handing him the phone.

"Hi," he answered.

"Timmy? This is Bob Kendall, the reporter. Remember me?"

"Yeah, sure."

"I've been checking on your friend. Haven't found out much. I talked with the owner of that property—he doesn't know anything about her. Cares less."

"Have you seen her?"

"Sure have. She's getting along. She's paralyzed on her left side—can't speak very well. Want to go with me this Saturday and visit her?"

"You bet!"

"O.K. I'll pick you up about ten a.m. Is that o.k.?"

Timmy agreed. He hoped his parents wouldn't interfere. He wouldn't tell them so they couldn't tell him he couldn't go. He wondered if the Old Lady would know him. Would she be mad because he'd interfered? What else could he have done?"

On Saturday, he wore his usual jeans but he had on a shirt and a sleeveless sweater. His mother commented, "Where are you going?"

"No place."

"That's not the way you dress to hang around."

"Well, if maybe Brian comes over, we're going to see a girl he knows."

"A girl? Tim, I don't want you to go with girls when you're only nine!"

"I'm not. Brian is. I'm just back up."

He settled down to play his Nintendo. The hands on the clock crawled with aggravating slowness. He was afraid his mother would drag him shopping or something.

"Tim, when do you expect Brian?"

"I dunno. 'Bout ten, I think."

"Well, I'm going shopping. Do you mind' being left alone?"

"Nope." Goodie, he thought.

"Your father's playing golf. He'll be back about noon, but I may not be. You can help him get lunch. There's makings for sandwiches and soup in the kitchen."

"We'll manage."

"All right. I'm leaving now." She left. Now the coast was clear. He waited until he heard the car backing out the driveway and then dashed to the porch to wait. It took forever before the reporter's car slid into the curb.

Timmy ran down the steps after carefully closing the house door. "I was lucky. Both

The Hermit

Mom and Dad are out. I was afraid they'd say something."

"I don't want to get you in trouble."

"I'm not. They don't know I'm going to see her."

"They don't like for you to go?" The reporter looked at Tim, troubled.

"Oh, it's o.k."

Doubtfully the reporter started the car and decided on a new tack. "Don't expect too much. She can't talk very well."

"She never did talk much."

"She may not remember you."

"That's o.k. I remember her."

They rode in silence and then Timmy asked, "Is everybody afraid?"

"What do you mean? Probably everybody has something to be scared of. Is that what you mean?"

"Not exactly. She said because people lived in houses, that showed they were afraid."

"I think most people live in houses because it's more comfortable."

"Yeah, I guess. I was going to ask Dad once, but our house is protected by a security company. Doesn't that mean he's afraid?"

"It could mean that—or he's cautious. Y'know, Tim, when people get possessions, they're afraid they may lose them. Now your friend didn't have any, so she couldn't lose anything. But she was afraid you'd tell somebody about her and that scared her."

Timmy thought carefully and said ruefully, "And I did, didn't I?"

"Yes, but you did it for a good reason. She needed help."

Timmy looked at his friend. "Do you think she'll mind?"

"She may. Here we are. We'll go in and find out."

"This isn't the hospital."

"It's the nursing home, in connection with the hospital. It's where she is now."

The happiness Timmy had felt on planning to see her had evaporated. He felt ashamed that he'd betrayed her, and his feet dragged. He didn't want her to yell at him.

They went up in the elevator and Timmy felt Kendall clutch his shoulder as they got to the fourth floor. "Down this way, Room 456."

When they entered her room, Timmy saw she still had a tube in her arm, but not the one in her nose. Her eyes were closed as he approached the bed.

"Hi. Remember me?"

Her eyes slitted open and then closed. He turned to the reporter. "I don't think she does."

He reached out and touched her hand. "Dog's living in our garage. I'm glad you're better."

Kendall came up. "You're listed as Jane Doe. So I'll call you Jane. Is that all right?"

There was no response. He continued. "Can you tell me your real name?"

She opened her eyes and looked at him silently. He continued, "This boy saved your life, you know."

She turned her eyes on Timmy. Her lips moved and Timmy leaned forward to hear. "Say it again. I wasn't listening hard." She spoke a garbled word.

"Why?" he repeated surprised. Her eyes

blinked. "Because you needed to be saved!"

Tears trickled down her thin cheeks. Her hand lifted and waved feebly, indicating she wanted them to leave.

"You want us to go?" Timmy asked. She blinked. "O.K. I'm glad you're better." Timmy went to the door, the reporter following.

Outside, Timmy said, "She didn't remember me. She's mad I sent her to the hospital."

"She has something she doesn't want anyone to know."

"What?"

"I don't know. That's the mystery we're going to have to solve." They went to the car. "How about we go out to her house? When do you have to be back?"

"Doesn't matter."

It seemed like a long time ago he had ridden up that hill and trudged down that path. At the house, the reporter paused in the doorway. "How could she live here?"

"I think she liked it," Timmy said. "At least in summer."

The reporter moved around touching things. "All she had were discards from the dump."

He went over to the crate that housed her cracked dish and chipped cup. A newspaper lined the shelf of the box. He slid it out.

"My mother always lined shelves. Surprises me your friend bothered."

He folded the newspaper and carried it absently as they walked back to his car. He dropped it on the seat.

"Well, that netted us nothing. Better get you home before your parents tell the police you're missing."

Timmy laughed with him.

Chapter Eight

It was Timmy who stumbled on the first clue.
As he was riding home with Bob Kendall, after
a visit at the nursing home, he disconsolate-
ly picked up a tossed newspaper in the back
seat. He was not really reading it, he was
using it as a blind against his sadness that
he had betrayed his friend. Carelessly his
eye caught the date on the paper.

"This is the paper that was in her box,
isn't it?"

"Yeah, guess so. "'S been floating around
in the back seat all this time."

"Why do you suppose she kept it?"

Bob shrugged and then he looked across at
the boy sharply. "You may have something
there. Why did she?" He turned over to the
curb, muttering, "My mother lined shelves
with newspaper. I just never thought. It was
strange your friend did."

There were two sheets in the fragment of
newspaper and Kendall took one and Timmy the
other.

"Read it," the reporter said, "and see if

you can see anything that can help."

The two skimmed over the paper in silence and Timmy finally said, "I don't see anything. What am I looking for?"

"Can't tell you. I haven't found anything either."

"Only thing I saw, somebody got out on parole an' the paper didn't like it."

"Who was it? Not Manson, I hope."

"No, some woman." Bob grabbed the paper and read:

"Cynthia Gray, convicted for drug possession and drugs for sale, and the suspicious death of a known drug dealer, has been released on parole. Ronald Traybold was instrumental in helping the police solve this murder case ten years ago. This is an example of questionable practices of parole. In her defense ten years ago, she claimed she was innocent, that it was Ronald Traybold who was guilty, casting dastardly aspersion on this distinguished family. Mr. Traybold, the scion of local Aaron Traybold, the late judge of the State Supreme Court who had served meritoriously on several federal committees, had many people who testified on his behalf that he was not a drug user and was being maliciously maligned by a local prostitute, Cynthia Gray. Mr. Traybold, Senior, has been dead for five years. His widow, a woman in her eighties, refused to be interviewed.

"My friend wasn't in prison!" Timmy protested. "That says some woman killed someone. My friend wouldn't do that!"

The Hermit

Bob was quiet as he restarted the car.

"It isn't her! I won't believe that!"

To calm him, the reporter said gently, "It's been known that innocent people have been sent to jail, Tim. Don't be so upset. You know it's a possible lead. How do we pursue it?"

"Ask her. She'll tell you it's not true."

The reporter grinned at the boy. "Think so, huh? She can't talk."

Shamefacedly, Timmy grinned in acknowledgement.

Kendall looked out at the passing traffic, tapping on the steering wheel. "Not very likely the Traybold woman would help. What's the date of that paper?"

"August 13, 1996."

"She served ten years. We could check the newspapers for 1986. Maybe we could find out just what took took place. Why if she got out on parole would she be hiding now? It's possible she had some family in court. Is that a local newspaper?"

"Nope, Atlanta," Timmy answered.

The reporter ruminated aloud. "She didn't want to be found.   Wonder why?"

Tears dripped down Timmy's cheek. It occurred to him to tear up the newspaper but the reporter had tossed it into the back seat. He couldn't believe his friend had been in prison.

"I have a friend in Atlanta. Maybe I can get some more information," Bob Kendall said as he started the car. "You're a good detective, kid."

Timmy was too miserable to answer.

"If I get any information, I'll give you a call. Are you going back to see the old lady?"

47

"No. Never again."

"Don't be so hard on her." Kendall steered to the curb at Timmy's house. "Keep up the good work, kid. Thanks for the lead."

Timmy left the car reluctantly. He liked Kendall. He didn't treat him like a kid. From the way they parted, he was afraid he would not see him again.

Chapter Nine

"Why aren't you eating, Timmy?" his mother asked.

"Guess I'm not hungry."

His mother looked at him with concern. "You went with that reporter again, didn't you? There's nothing good that can come with talking to a reporter."

"Yeah, I went with him. He's nice."

"To visit that old woman? I wish you wouldn't. It upsets you so."

Timmy said nothing.

"Did you see her?" At his nod, his mother continued. "How is she? Is she getting well?"

The boy's face clouded. "She hates me. She wishes I hadn't sent for the ambulance."

"Well she and I agree."

"She was sick!"

"It wasn't your business. You weren't even supposed to be up there."

"You said we were supposed to help people!"

"She doesn't think you helped her, does she?"

Timmy miserably shook his head. He got up.

Elizabeth H. Noble

"I'm going to take Dog for a walk." Angrily he turned on his mother.

"I s'pose you think I should take Dog back and just leave him up there alone."

"It has occurred to me." She was picking up the lunch plates and handling them roughly. "Your disobedience hasn't helped anyone, including you."

Timmy walked out without comment. It was true. The old lady did not want to talk with him. Dog was not happy being confined. He couldn't even walk freely, but had to have Timmy on one end of the leash. I've certainly made a mess of things, he thought, patting the broad head at his side. Now the reporter was trying to find out if the woman in the paper was his friend. Had she been in prison? She could have been. This would really make his parents mad.

Anyway, he probably wouldn't see his reporter friend again, either. Everything was all crooked and terrible. He tried to remember the fun of making it to the top of the hill with his bike, and he couldn't feel it again. He tried to remember being with his friend, but now that seemed misty and pointless.

"You're the only thing I have," he said to the dog. As he walked on, he added, "and I guess I'm the only thing you've got." It was small consolation. Tomorrow he'd try to go see his friend again. The reporter thought he could get in alone now that she was in a nursing home.

But if she didn't want to see him, what good was that? He struggled to remember his visits with her during the summer. She was teaching him something, making him see things differently. If he could do that for her— would that help? He determined to see her again. He started to run with Dog but had to stop as Dog kept running faster and faster and he couldn't keep up. But at least he knew what he was going to do Saturday. He would go to the nursing home. He'd heard about dogs in nursing homes. Maybe he could get Dog in.

Chapter Ten

At the nursing home, Timmy entered, Dog on a short leash. Should he ask or just plow on? "If your parents might not like something, just do it, don't ask. You can apologize afterwards," Brian had advised him so Timmy walked to the elevator.

That elevator was too crowded. He waited for the next one and then entered. Dog stood quietly, lazily waving his tail as two or three people got on.

At his friend's floor, Timmy got out. A nurse confronted him. "What do you have there?" she asked.

"A dog. I'm visiting my friend—it's her dog. She wants to see him."

The nurse turned away to ask someone else and Timmy hurried to his friend's room. He went in. She was lying there, as she usually was, with closed eyes. Dog made a deep agonized noise in his throat and leaped on the bed. He nuzzled the woman, crying in his happiness at seeing her again. It was then the nurse hurried in.

"Get that animal off the bed!" Timmy struggled to pull Dog off.

"We do allow small animals, but not a monster like that. Get it off the bed!"

"I'm trying."

The nurse reached out and grabbed the leash, gave a yank and Dog, slipping on the sheets, was dragged off, taking the sheets with him.

The nurse hastily pulled the bed back together again. "Don't you dare bring that beast in here again."

"Dog," said the woman, her right arm groping.

Dog propelled Timmy to the side of the bed so he could lick the old hand.

The nurse stopped grumbling and looked at her patient. Tears were sliding down the woman's cheeks. "Dog," she said again. Her fingers curled up and stroked the dog's chin as he nosed her hand.

"That's the first reaction she's ever made," the nurse said, "but don't let him get on the bed again. We can't have that."

"I brought Dog to see you," Timmy said, moving around the bed. "Are you feeling better? Can you talk to me?"

The old woman just kept repeating, "Dog, Dog." It surprised Timmy. He did not remember her paying much attention to the dog when he had visited her. She did not speak to him, but her hand fondled the dog as he stood patiently by.

"We're trying to find out who you are," Timmy offered. The old woman paid him no attention. Her tears were still trailing down her cheek and her hand moved over the dog's black face. She kept repeating, softly, "Dog, Dog."

"We're going to help you. I'll bring Dog again. Don't cry."

He did not know what else to say so he started dragging resisting Dog toward the door.

"Dog" At her voice, Dog started back, dragging Timmy behind him. And then Dog barked, his powerful voice shattering the quietness.

The nurse came rushing back in. "What are you doing?"

"She doesn't want Dog to leave," Timmy said, still struggling to get the dog under control. To his friend he called, "I'll bring him again. I won't forget."

The nurse joined him, yanking on the leash and together she and the boy dragged the panting dog to the door. She pushed them out and shut the door. Dog reared against the door, forcing it open, but the nurse slammed it shut.

"Come on, Dog. We've got to go." With another bay of indignation, Dog flopped to the floor. Timmy tried to drag him but couldn't. Looping the leash over his arm, he bent down and rolled the dog over and then again.

Somebody laughed and said, "What are you trying to do?"

"Get the dog out. He wants to stay, his owner's in there."

The voice belonged to a big black man. "Here, let me help." He took the leash and pulled. Dog stayed put, giving a low growl.

"Will he bite?"

"No," Timmy answered with a confidence he did not have. He grabbed the collar and with the black man's pulling the dog upright, the two got him to the elevator.

"That's too big a dog for you," the man said.

"It's just he hasn't seen her for so long." The elevator opened and gobbled them up for their trip downstairs and outside. Dog padded along side the boy, resigned.

Chapter Eleven

Timmy was surprised the following Thursday to be called by Bob Kendall.

"Timmy? Are you ready to go visit our friend in the nursing home?"

"Yeah. I want to take Dog to visit her. I did last week."

"They let that monster in?"

Timmy muttered, "They weren't pleased."

"O.K., you, me and Dog. About three?"

"You know something?"

"Want to check with her. See you?"

"You bet."

Timmy hesitated about asking permission to go. He knew his parents didn't like him to see the reporter.

As Saturday approached, he hoped desperately they would both have plans for Saturday.

But he finally said to his mother when they were washing supper dishes, "Mr. Kendall's asked me to go with him, Saturday."

"Who's Mr. Kendall?" she asked as she plunged dishes into the soapy water. "Is that your teacher?"

Timmy shook his head and picked up the dish towel. "He's that reporter, remember. You kept the article he wrote about me."

"The reporter? Oh, yes. What's he doing with you?"

Timmy carefully laid the dried dish on the kitchen table. "I think he wants to go see the Old Lady and asked me to bring Dog."

"Why are you getting mixed up in this? You know I don't like your getting involved."

"Well, I feel—I know she didn't want people to know where she lived and now people do. I feel responsible."

"Well wouldn't she be most unhappy to have a reporter visit her?"

"That's why I have to take Dog. She likes Dog."

"I really don't like this, Timmy."

"Mr. Kendall's nice. Why don't you like him?"

His mother thought for awhile and then she laughed. "My mother said the only time a lady should have her name in the paper was when she was born, when she married and when she died. I guess that's why I feel you shouldn't be seeing that reporter. Do you like him?"

"Yeah, I guess. He doesn't treat me like a kid. And he's helped me see her in the hospital."

His mother took a long time soaping the next dish and rinsing it off. "I'm glad you asked me, Timmy. I don't really like it, but I appreciate your telling me. You may go with this Mr. Kendall."

"Oh, thank you, Mom!" Timmy took the dried plates to the cupboard. "Thanks.

"It means a lot to you, doesn't it, Timmy?"

The Hermit

"Yeah—sorta makes me feel grown up."

She smiled at him and nothing more on the subject was said.

When they met that Saturday, Dog seated uneasily in back, Bob said, "Tim, you remember that newspaper clipping?"

"Yeah, It's not her, is it? I don't want her to have been in prison."

"I was checking with my friend down in Atlanta. There was a drug trial, and she was convicted—by the man she was living with at the time."

Timmy slouched in his seat. "Drugs."

"If it makes you feel any better, I think maybe she was railroaded, but yes, for drugs and later for murder she was in prison. "

"Let's not bring it up."

"Don't you want to know?"

"Not if that's it." He fiddled with a piece of paper he'd found in his pocket. "I liked her. She was just a person who was different. Let's leave it that way."

Timmy did not hear his friend's muttered, "I can't do that, kid." They drove in silence to the nursing home.

There, Dog jumped out happily. He remembered the place. He dragged Timmy to the door. The three of them went in, Bob's hand helping with the leash. When they got off the elevator, the nurse recognized the dog. "You can go in, but no dog on the bed."

Timmy raised his hand in acknowledgement. When they went into the room, Dog's nails scratched on the floor as he pulled Timmy to the bed.

The old woman roused and at the touch of Dog's tongue, cried out, "Dog!"

Timmy and Bob stood silently by the bed as they watched. Finally Bob said softly, "Cynthia?"

The woman made no response, just saying softly, "Dog, dog." Dog was whimpering, nuzzling her.

Timmy pushed forward.

"I used to visit you. Remember? We picked berries—and weeds together."

For a moment her eyes focused on him and then skittered back to the mastiff.

Timmy retreated and said sadly to Bob, "She doesn't remember me."

"Maybe she doesn't want to. The dog is safe—he can't talk and probably didn't know her before. She doesn't want anyone to know her."

"You're going to tell, aren't you?"

"So far I don't have anything to tell. It's a hunch, that's all."

"I don't want to come again. C'mon, Dog." Timmy yanked on the leash but the dog was bigger than he.

Kendall reached out and touched the woman's hand. "Are you Cynthia?"

"Dog."

"She wants us to leave Dog," Timmy guessed.

"We can't. We'll come again."

Mournfully she reiterated, "Dog, dog."

Bob and Timmy pulled a protesting Dog to the elevator.

At the car, after struggling with the reluctant animal but finally getting him in the car, Bob got in the driver's seat. He looked down at Timmy.

"She's getting better, Timmy. I think she knows who she is—who you are."

The Hermit

Timmy's face was woodenly turned to his window. "Let's go. I'm not coming again."

"Dog helped her."

"I'm not betraying her again."

Chapter Twelve

Bob Kendall strode into the nursing home. After some asking, he found Timmy's friend in the solarium. She was sitting in a wheel chair staring glumly out the window.

"Cynthia?" he addressed her. She made no move. "Cynthia Gray?"

There was no indication she heard him.

He approached her, touched her hand, and said, "I think you're Cynthia Gray. You hooked up with Ronald Traybold. a big family name in Atlanta. But he was on drugs and was dragging you down. And then he was fingered for drug dealing and murder, convinced the police it was you who was doing the drug dealing. He had money and power and you had nothing. So you were charged. You got out on parole three or four years ago and have been hiding out since. But if you'd been paroled, why are you hiding now?"

Her wooden face gave no indication she even heard him.

"Am I right?" Is that how it happened? Our young friend Timmy is pretty upset. He refuses to believe you were ever involved in drugs and even murder. You weren't were you? He's right. Let me help you get this stuff cleared up and you can reenter society."

There was no reaction. He reached out and touched her again. She jerked her arm free. "Speak to me, Cynthia. Now that I've found you, let me help you."

She turned angry eyes on him and painfully rose from the chair and gripping chairs, door jambs, and hall walls, she staggered her way out of the solarium. Hastily Bob Kendall grabbed the wheel chair and pursued her. He reached her and gently guided her back into the chair.

"I don't think you're ready to take off just yet." He wheeled her to her room and helped her out of the chair and onto the bed. "We're really your friends. Help us."

She glared at him. He pulled the covers up around her. "But if you were out on parole, why were you hiding? He could tell she was still agitated so he said, " Take it easy. You're safe here."

As he went out, he stopped at the desk. "Keep an eye on Jane Doe. I think she's planning to escape." They laughed.

As he walked to his car he thought, Why would she hide out after she had gotten out on parole? She might have been anathema in Atlanta, but she could have moved some place else. Well, I guess she'd have to have money—herself or family. So far I haven't tracked down family. But it doesn't make sense.

As he got in the car he said to himself, I'd better contact Atlanta again. There must be something else. Is this Ronald Traybold still around? Do you suppose she killed him? Does he want to kill her? There must be some reason she's so scared of being found. He wondered if his paper would send him down to Georgia. Not if he didn't have more than he did right now. There wasn't much use talking to Timmy, even if Timmy would talk to him. He was pretty adamant about not going to the nursing home again. Like the rest of us, Bob thought, he's washed his hands of Cynthia Gray.

Chapter Thirteen

Timmy was miserable. He sat on the steps
stroking Dog's head. "I just don't want to
see her. Not when she's been in jail and all—
especially for killing someone. It doesn't
make any difference to you, I know. Guess I'm
not as good as dogs. You keep looking at me
as if asking when I'm taking you to see her
again. Well, I'm not. You're just goin' to
have to forget her the way I am."

The trouble was, he couldn't.

His mother came to the kitchen door.
"Timmy, you should come in. It's too chilly
out there."

"I'm o.k." He did not turn around or look
at his mother.

She came out, arms crossed and clenched
against the chill. "Timmy, I want you inside.
You know we're going to have to do something
about that dog. He eats like a horse and your
father isn't happy having him here."

"Do something—what do you mean?"

"I'm afraid it will be the Humane Society.
Mastiffs are valuable. Someone will adopt him."

Timmy abruptly stood up. "You can't do that. He belongs to my friend. You can't give him away."

His mother took the opportunity to usher him into the house, "She may never get well enough again to live on her own." She reacted to the boy's shocked look. "Timmy, she was practically starving and she is old and she won't recover easily."

"But you can't give Dog away! He's hers."

His mother turned away to the cupboard. "Here are some cookies. Have you done your homework?"

In a flash Timmy had whirled and was out the door. He untied Dog and ran to the garage and got on his bicycle. Riding the bike and holding the rope by which Dog had been tied, he started up the hill back to the old lady's house. Dog loped comfortably beside him. Shortly Timmy was trudging up the hill, supporting the bike with one hand and keeping hold of Dog with the other. He had certainly gotten in a mess. Finally he untied Dog and the animal trotted into the field. Maybe he should just leave him here. It's the way he had lived with the old lady—he'd fed himself. At least he wouldn't be given away. Would being adopted be so bad? Maybe he wouldn't mind that—having his food brought to him; not having to hunt for it. Maybe people would like him. Was he being selfish to deny a home to Dog? But he belonged to the old lady.

Timmy stopped walking. He stood there, bracing his bike upright and looking at Dog sniffing through bushes. The dog, sensing his stopping turned and looked at him and trotted back. Timmy rubbed the soft ears. "It would-

n't be fair to give you away before you had
a chance to see her again." But then he
thought, "They might take you away tomorrow
while I'm in school. You wouldn't even know
what was happening to you. Dog, what should I
do?" Dog reared up on him and licked him with
a sympathetic tongue.

Slowly Timmy started again up the hill, Dog
staying close. "I can't let them take you
away tomorrow. We'll go on and stay at her
house overnight. Then tomorrow I'll take you
to the nursing home and she can say good bye
to you."

It seemed a good plan. Timmy rode down hill
on the bike but it was getting dark. He got
off, walking along the roadside so he could
see the faint path the woman and Dog had worn
to her house.

"It's going to be scary in that house
tonight," Timmy mused. He reached out and
clutched the new collar that his father had
bought for the dog. At least Dog would be with
him. He had never been at the house at night.
Would bats be flying around there?

He spotted the trail and turned down it. It
wasn't so dark as he had thought it would be.
His eyes had grown accustomed to the gloom
and now stars were peeking out and he could
see the dim outlines of the path. It seemed
an awful long time before he got to the house.
"Do you s'pose it's fallen down?" he asked
Dog. Dog was moving faster and Timmy fell
trying to keep up with him. It hurt his knee
but he got up. Dog was waiting for him. Dog
trotted ahead and the house was suddenly
looming. Dog entered, tail waving.

Timmy stumbled in. It was dark and unwelcoming. Dog jumped on the rigged bed. He seemed at home. Timmy sat down beside him and shivered.

"It's cold and I'm hungry. Should have grabbed some cookies."

He curled up by Dog and started shivering. Hesitatingly he clawed back the bedclothes. They were torn, dirty and smelled but he crawled inside and invited Dog in. Hugging Dog to him, "We'll go back tomorrow, and I'll take you to the nursing home again. Then I'll let them take you to be adopted. Do you want a new home?" Dog nuzzled him.

Timmy lay cold and afraid. Dog went to sleep, his head a comforting weight on Timmy's stomach.

Chapter Fourteen

Timmy leaped up as somebody towered over him snarling, "What the hell?" The boy froze in silence. Dog was not. He was growling fiercely, standing over the boy's feet, challenging the intruder.

The man stepped back. "Who in hell are you?"

Timmy retreated under the covers, but he answered, "I'm her friend."

"Ain't nobody here."

"She was."

"Why're you here?"

Timmy could not think of any reason that was credible.

"Why are YOU?" he countered. "Who are you?"

"'s raining." The man withdrew and Dog laid down on Timmy's feet but remained alert.

It was dark in the room. Timmy could no longer see the man. He wondered if it were raining. It was dark, but he was not sure what time it was.

And then the rough voice came again. "Whacha know about her?"

Timmy hesitated. "Not much."

"What?"

Timmy didn't know whether he wanted the answer repeated, or if he wanted to know what Timmy knew. He said cautiously, "Not much."

"Name?" Timmy ducked, "Timmy Hasting."

"Hers."

"She never told me."

"Why ya here?"

Once again Timmy explored reasons and elected silence. "Your dog?"

"Not really. Hers."

"Where's she?"

"In a hospital."

"Why?"

"I think she had a stroke."

"Dead?"

"No."

"How long she's been gone?"

"'Bout a month."

There were no more questions. Timmy tried to keep his fear under control. Who was this man?

He lay rigid in silence. At last he could see the outside door and watched as light seeped around it. It wasn't bright but it was morning. Cautiously he stuck his feet out from under the covers. He looked carefully around. There was a brown ungainly hump—the man? Asleep? Would he be able to sneak out the door? Dog got off the bed and stalked over to the brown heap.

"Dog!" Timmy hissed.

Dog did not listen. He approached the brown bunch of rags and sniffed, a low growl sounding in his throat.

The Hermit

"Dog!" a whispered order. Timmy made for the outside door.

Too late. "Hey, you!"

Timmy froze.

"Call your damned mutt."

"Why?"

The brown heap had rolled over and scrambled to his feet.

"Where yuh think you're goin'?"

Dog's growl rumbled.

"Home. C'mon, Dog."

Dog braced his legs and faced the man. The tramp flourished a fist. "Git back here!"

Dog leaped, taking the man to the floor and holding him down.

Timmy hovered by the door. "We're going, Dog. C'mon." Timmy bolted for the door and ran out. Outside he ran frantically down the path and then stopped. He'd left Dog. How could he leave Dog? He turned and went back.

The man was still immobile on the floor, the dog standing on his chest, muzzle close to the terrified face.

"Dog, come here." Dog paid no attention. After a moment, the place in complete silence, Timmy said, "I'll come get him if you let me go."

"O.K." It was a muffled answer.

Timmy ran up, grabbed Dog's collar and yanked hard. The dog came, protesting. With the dog securely by the collar, Timmy turned and started for the door. Immediately a big hand reached out and hurled him backward. "Not so fast, kid."

Dog leaped again on the man and pinned him to the floor, his growls threatening.

Elizabeth H. Noble

"You promised," Timmy protested. "You want me to leave you with Dog?"

"Ya tell me . . .." The man lifted an arm to push the dog away but Dog caught it in his teeth. The man let out a banshee scream.

"Dog!"

Dog ignored Timmy, glaring down at the man. The man spoke.

"Where's the stuff?"

"What stuff? She didn't have anything."

"Hell, she didn't. We all knew she did."

"If she lived here, do you think she had money?" Timmy's disbelief was evident.

"Get this damned dog off me."

"You'll grab me again."

The outside door banged open. Timmy whirled.

"Thank God I've found you!" Mr. Hastings hugged his son. "We were so"—he saw the dog and the man. "What's this?"

"I don't know who he is. He came in last night and was going to grab me but Dog won't let him."

Mr. Hastings pulled his cell phone out of his pocket and dialed 911. "I need the police immediately .. . . My dog has trapped an intruder. . .Yes, I think I can hold him for a while." He quickly gave directions for the police and hung up.

"Who are you?" he asked the man.

"Call off your damned dog."

"No, I think he's doing a good job just as he is. What did you want with my son?"

"Nothin'. It was raining. I just came in."

Mr. Hastings looked at his son, the boy shrugged.

"My son said you grabbed him."

The Hermit

"Naw. Didn't know he was here."

"Odd that the dog jumped you."

"He's vicious—shouldn't be loose. Get him off'n me!"

"My son was leaving and you grabbed him. Why?"

There wasn't an answer. Mr. Hastings turned to his son.

"Why did you come up here?"

"Mom was going to give Dog away. You can't do that when he isn't your dog."

"I'm glad he was with you. How come you came up here, though?"

"I was thinking of leaving Dog here. When he lived here with the old lady, he fed himself—hunting."

"And?"

"It was getting dark, so I just stayed."

"Probably pretty sensible. You know your mother is frantic."

Tim stood there mutely, head down.

"Nothing that can't be repaired," his father said, circling him with his arm and hugging him.

Tim said thoughtfully, "I'd about decided that Dog might like to be adopted and have a family that cared about him."

"I think after this, he probably has."

It took a while before Timmy understood. He looked up. "You mean us?"

His father nodded. They heard the sound of a car and went to the door. It was the police. Timmy went and, backed by the police, dragged Dog off the tramp.

Mr. Hastings was instructed to go to the police station to press charges and the protesting bum was thrust into the police car.

"Hard to say he was trespassing when we don't even own the place," Mr. Hastings muttered to Timmy. "Did he hurt you in any way, threaten you, bother you?"

"He bothered me—I was scared but except for throwing me down when I was leaving, there wasn't anything. He did ask me where she had the 'stuff. I don't know what he was talking about."

"What stuff?" Timmy shrugged and shook his head.

"Well, I don't think there are any charges to be made against him. So we'll go down and tell them to let him go."

"I'm glad you said we could keep Dog." Timmy relaxed in the car seat. His eyes were closing when he murmured, "I promised Dog I'd take him to see her again."

Chapter Fifteen

Mr. Hastings and Timmy had just entered the police station when Timmy saw Bob, the reporter.

"Hi, why are you here?"

"Checking for stories. What are you doing here?"

"I was up at the old lady's house—I'd taken Dog up there an' it got dark so I stayed overnight."

Bob looked at the boy in surprise. "You must be a brave person. That house is creepy in the daylight—say nothing of the dark."

"Then a tramp came in and that scared me."

"A tramp? That house is pretty far out. What did he want?"

"He said he wanted her stuff—anyway he asked where her stuff was."

"What stuff?"

Timmy shrugged.

"Think I'll talk to him."

"Dad said he wouldn't charge him with any-thing—they'd let him go." The boy looked over at his father at the desk.

"Good, he's still here. I'll grab him on the way out."

The two waited until the tramp was escorted to the desk. Bob approached him. "You knew Cynthia Gray? How did you know her?" he asked the tramp.

"Don' know who yer talkin' 'bout." The tramp tried to brush past the reporter.

"You said she had some "stuff". What sort of stuff?" The reporter dragged the man over to the side. "Are we talking drugs?"

"Naw." The tramp tried to squirm away. "Don' know any—whatever you said."

"She may not have used that name. You were at her house."

The tramp burst away and started for the door, Bob after him.

"What's going on, Tim?" Mr. Hastings asked.

"He wanted to talk to the tramp. I told him he'd ask me where the "stuff" was."

"Well, come on, let's go home."

Timmy craned his neck to see the tramp and Bob Kendall but he couldn't hear anything—just saw the tramp struggling to get away and Roberts trying to hold him.

"Dad, let's go over there," he urged.

"Best to stay out of it, son. Kendall's a reporter—we don't want to get mixed up with him."

"But I want to know about her."

"It's over, Tim. You have your dog, she's being treated in a hospital. There's nothing to be gained by pushing further."

Chapter Sixteen

Now that he was assured that Dog would not be spirited away, Timmy felt less urgency and more reluctance to take Dog to see the old lady. But finally on Saturday he decided he would have to keep his promise to Dog.

His father had used the brisk weather as an excuse to get in one more game of golf and his mother was making out a list to go grocery shopping.

"Mom, I'm gong to Brian's."

"I thought you could go shopping with me."

Timmy scuffed one foot and didn't answer.

His mother looked up and sighed. "O.K., but be back before five—earlier if Brian's called in to supper." She went back to her list, saying softly, "I'll miss you."

Timmy hastily left, feeling doubly guilty for his lie and disappointing his mother. He used to love to go to the store with her, it usually meant a treat they shared, but he wanted to get over his last visit to the old lady.

He leashed up Dog and started on foot to the hospital, running the first block so that his mother wouldn't see him on her way to the store. Dog pulled, eager to run.

When they got to the nursing home, Tim gripped the leash so that it was short and he had tight control of the dog. He'd been allowed to bring the dog, but some of the nurses objected. He hoped he would duck those ones. He carefully chose an empty elevator and Dog stood by him gently waving his tail. At the floor, Timmy went out carefully ducking the nurse's station. He went to her room and looked in. She wasn't there. No one was. He'd have to confront a nurse after all. What had Bob Kendall called her? Jane Something. Jane. . . . Timmy groped for the name and then he was at the nurse's desk and it suddenly popped into his head.

"I'm looking for Jane Doe." Dog was hugged close to him and he hoped the nurse wouldn't see him.

"Ah, our mystery patient." The nurse looked up at him critically. He'd never seen her before. "Who's with you?" she asked.

Timmy wished Bob Kendall was, but he mummbled, "No one."

The nurse turned to someone behind a partition. "Can kids come in alone?"

A familiar nurse stuck her head out. "He's been here before. Have the elephant with you?" she asked Timmy.

He nodded and hoped they wouldn't notice. The familiar nurse said, "Look in the Solarium, end of the floor. We rolled her down there after lunch."

Timmy and Dog plodded down to the sunny room at the end of the hall. He stood there, holding tightly to Dog's leash. There were

several wheel chairs there with people slump-
ing indolently in them. Most were asleep, but
he saw two women talking and then he saw the
old lady. She was apart from everyone else,
her nose sharper and longer and her chin
looking more witch-like than ever. Her eyes
were closed. Dog, quicker than Timmy, had
started pulling toward her.

The two went over, Dog's toenails scratch-
ing the floor in his eagerness to get to her.

"Lady," Timmy began hesitantly, but Dog was
licking her hand and she rasped, "Dog, Dog."

Timmy started again. "I'll keep Dog for you
until you're well." That wasn't really accu-
rate, and he stumbled on. "I was afraid they
were going to take him to the Humane Society
and I went up to your place."

She ignored him and just kept repeating,
"Dog, Dog." Dog tried to get in her lap, but
was tugged down.

Timmy continued, bound to tell her the
truth though she didn't seem interested in
anything but Dog. "A tramp came in and Dog
protected me, so Dad said we could keep him."
Her eyes glanced sharply at him and then went
back to Dog. Quickly he added, "Until you're
well, of course." He knew that was a lie. His
family had never planned for him to see the
old lady again.

Dog was crying in his joy at seeing the old
woman. Her hand smoothed his head and ears
and she kept repeating "Dog, dog."

"How are you?" Timmy asked, uncomfortable
with her silence. He wondered if she could
say anything other than 'dog'. She did not
answer and he asked softly, "Are you real mad
at me?"

Again she did not respond. Defeated, Timmy sank to the floor, keeping Dog on a tight rein, but still within her range.

Finally he tried again and asked, "Is your name Cynthia Gray?"

She did not answer nor look at him but her hand gripped Dog's ear for a moment and then continued sliding across his head. Timmy thought dismally, "That's who she is."

He stood up. "I probably won't see you again. Good bye." He pulled Dog away and her hand tried to follow but Dog was too far away. She closed her eyes, but Timmy saw a tear start down her cheek. "For Dog," he thought and turned and left.

Chapter Seventeen

About a week later, Timmy came home and saw Bob Kendall's shabby car at the curb. He went up eagerly. Kendall got out of the car to meet him.

"How'r ya doing?" he asked as Timmy came up.

"Who was the tramp?" Timmy dove in directly.

"You mean what was his connection? Well after our friend Carolyn Gray got out of prison, she drifted and he met her then. He paid her to buy dope for him and she ran. I don't know how he tracked her down. He wouldn't tell me."

"I don't want to hear." Timmy started up his sidewalk.

"She didn't buy the stuff, kid. Don't be so hard on her. Have you seen her?"

"Not going to," Timmy did not turn around.

"I'm going this Saturday. Want to come?"

Timmy shook his head. But he had stopped walking.

"I think she was framed. I don't think she was guilty of anything. Don't be so hard on her."

Timmy turned an anguished face toward the reporter. "I betrayed her, and now I've stolen her dog."

"You tried to help her, and she may never again be able to have Dog."

"That's what Mom said. But Dad said we could keep Dog because he protected me against the tramp."

"I can imagine. He told me what a vicious beast it was."

"Dog isn't vicious—just pinned him."

"Bet he could. You know that was what mastiffs were bred to do—guard places against poachers. They worked in pairs, one pinned and the other ran for help."

"Really? I wasn't much help. It was only because Dad came that I'm not still there." A brief grin flashed.

Bob Kendall said, "You're a brave kid. Come with me Saturday, will you? I think she'd rather talk to you than me."

"She doesn't talk. I tried. The only thing she says is 'dog'." He paused and then added, "I asked if she was Cynthia Gray and she didn't answer but I thought she acted as if it meant something."

"That's why I'd really like to have you go with me to the nursing home, Tim."

Timmy shook his head. "I really don't want to see her again." He turned toward the house, but threw back over his shoulder, "O.K. Pick me up."

The next Saturday, Bob Kendall came for Timmy and they went to the nursing home, with Dog. Timmy was still uncomfortable with the idea.

"Why are we going to see her?" he asked.

The Hermit

"In the first place, I want to see if she reacts to the tramp's name. At least the name he gave me, which might not be his right one."

"Why am I going?"

"Because you're her friend, and you have Dog. Dog's probably the only one she really wants to see," Kendall replied realistically.

They got out at the nursing home, Timmy dragging his feet but being pulled by Dog. Kendall pushed him ahead of him into the room. She was lying there on her bed, eyes closed, her inert left arm dangling, her right folded over her body. Dog rushed to the bed and licked the dangling hand.

"Dog," she said. Her eyes didn't open but her grim face did change.

"I came back," Timmy ventured. There was no response. Dog ducked around the bed and her hand found his head.

"Met a friend, maybe just an acquaintance of yours the other day," the reporter said. There was no response. He continued, "Said his name was Bob Watts." There was no appreciable reaction. "He'd dropped in at your house the other night when Timmy and the dog were there. Said he was just getting in out of the rain, but he knew it was your house."

Her eyes and face were closed.

After a moment, Timmy said, "I'm sorry I betrayed you. I just wanted to help you. You were sick."

"Knew." It was a rusty sound.

"New what?" Timmy answered, baffled.

"Y'came."

"What?"

"'N."

"I don't know what you're saying."

"I think she means that when you first came, she knew her isolation was ended," Kendall interpreted.

The fingers on her right hand raised from the dog's head and wiggled.

"But I wouldn't have told if you hadn't needed help."

She made no response.

"I'm sorry."

Her hand left Dog's head and reached outward. Kendall pushed Timmy so that she could touch the boy. She touched him briefly with her fingertips, eyes still closed. Timmy steeled himself not to flinch and then reached out and took the skeletal hand. "Thank you."

"Why did Bob Watts visit you?" Kendall asked.

There was no response.

"We don't want to tire you. I hope you realize we only want to help."

The eyelids opened and hate flashed. Timmy dropped her hand and backed away. Kendall reached forward and took her hand but she abruptly withdrew it. "Believe me," he said, "we are your friends. We'll go now and leave you in peace." He reached for Dog's leash and helped Timmy drag the protesting dog away and out the door.

In the car Kendall said, "Didn't get much that time, did we?"

Timmy said softly, "I think she forgave me."

"That she did." The reporter looked over at the boy. "That means a lot to you, doesn't it?" Timmy nodded, struggling against tears.

Chapter Eighteen

It was some comfort to Timmy that the Old Lady had forgiven him. He never used the name the reporter thought was hers. He did not want to think of that person. Just the person he had known who lived in solitude and ate just what God provided—providing she worked hard enough.

He never told his friends about the old lady. She was his secret. Once someone had seen him going into the nursing home, but he had lied and said he was visiting a friend of his father's. When they asked about Dog, he used this same mythical friend. They were keeping it for him. Apparently no one he knew read the newspapers. There had been that first article about his rescuing his sick friend. His mother had saved it, though she hadn't been pleased with him for the deed.

It was cold now and he and Dog did not go back to that decrepit old house. He wondered if the tramp was still there and if he had found the old lady's "stuff".

Elizabeth H. Noble

It was a Tuesday and he had been downtown when he saw Bob Kendall. Kendall had yelled at him and come over to talk.

"Guess what, Kid," Roberts greeted him. "Gotta friend from Atlanta coming up here. Thinks he might have known our elderly friend."

Timmy shrank from this news and didn't respond.

"Don't you really want to confirm who our old lady is?"

"She's not yours," Timmy answered hotly.

"Your old lady," the reporter hastily corrected. "You know, we might wind up this mystery yet."

Timmy turned and ran. He did not want to find out the truth. He only wanted his old idea—she was a hero. He didn't want her revealed as a criminal and running away from prison. But even as he ran, he knew he could not stop what was coming.

Surprisingly, Kendall called him a week later and said his Atlanta friend was here, and did Timmy want to go to the nursing home with them. Timmy did not want to, but to his amazement heard himself agreeing to go. When the two reporters came, he decided he could not back out so he crawled into the back seat and the two adults sat chatting in the front seat.

"It's really Timmy's discovery," Bob Kendall was explaining to his friend. "He found her, rescued her when he found her sick, and discovered the newspaper article which gave me the lead."

Timmy cowered into himself. Betrayed her, he thought.

The Hermit

When they got to the nursing home, he lagged behind the two men as they marched in. They stopped at her room, which was empty and Kendall led them to the Solarium. Timmy thought of dashing back to the car, but something dragged him along in the men's wake.

In the solarium, he saw her, but said nothing. Bob Kendall spotted her and strode over. She looked around him and saw Timmy and said, "Dog?"

"Not today," Timmy admitted. He had not thought of bringing the dog.

Kendall asked her how she was, but she turned away and did not respond. He told her about the tramp and she ignored him. Suddenly she released the brakes on her wheel chair and rolled away. She stopped by Timmy and put out her hand and touched him. He felt she meant to smile, but nothing but her eyes changed and she rolled on.

Kendall did not follow. He turned to his Atlanta friend and asked, "Is she the one?"

"Hard to tell. She's old and damaged by the stroke. Doesn't talk much, does she?"

"Is that contrary to what she was at the trial?"

"No, she offered nothing in her defense and responded not at all to her defense attorney."

"In character. Well, what do you think?"

The friend thought for a moment and he and Kendall, Timmy trailing, started for the elevator. "Couldn't swear it," he answered, "but I would guess she's our Cynthia Gray."

"Can you tell us about the case?" Roberts asked.

"Well, originally drug selling charges

were brought against Ronald Traybold, scion of the wealthy Traybold family of Atlanta. He wiggled out of them by charging this Cynthia Gray. Said he had been living with her, and she brought money into the house and he found out it was drug money. So he backed out and said that apparently in retaliation she had given his name to the Narcs. There was money behind him, and the family was prominent so she was charged and didn't fight very hard for herself and got sent to prison."

"Did you tell me Traybold was killed and she was charged? How could she kill him if she were in prison on a narcotics charge?"

"She'd gotten paroled. Had no money, apparently was homeless—easy to pick up, easy to prosecute."

"How did she kill him?"

"He was shot."

"Could she get hold of a gun and ammunition when she was a street person?"

"Probably. They never found the gun. The charge was based on motive...."

"Then the prosecutor believed she had been railroaded?"

"Well, I think there was a good deal of pressure by the Traybold family. She had been dumped by their son so it could have been avenging that. Besides, a prominent person had been killed and you know the media and political pressure exerted in that kind of case." The men were strolling along but Timmy listened, though he didn't interrupt. It didn't sound as if his Old Lady were so bad. Maybe she was innocent of everything. He began to feel a little better. Saturday, he decided, he'd take Dog to visit her.

Chapter Nineteen

Saturday Timmy decided to take Dog to see the Old Woman. His mother was on the phone and it was easy for him to slip away on his bike, Dog trailing along at the end of two leashes snapped together. There were not a lot of cars on the street and it was not too hard to get to the nursing home with Dog.

As usual he got up to her room without a problem. This time she was in her room and as usual Dog dashed over to greet her, exultantly putting his paws on the bed and licking her. She muttered "Dog" and her thin hand caressed his head.

"Good," she said, looking at Timmy.

He grinned and nodded agreement.

"Are you Cynthia Gray?" he asked. Her eyes became vacant and she just stroked Dog's head and said, "Dog."

Timmy wondered if she could say anything more, but just wouldn't. "My reporter friend says you're Cynthia Gray. Did you sell drugs, kill someone?"

"Dog," she answered, not looking at him.

"I don't think you did," Timmy continued, "but it would explain why you were hiding up in the hills." He waited for her to speak and noticed her eyes were closed. "Are you asleep?"

He waited for an answer of some kind—either words or the wave of her hand. He didn't think she was asleep as her hand was still rubbing Dog's ears, first one and then the other.

"Mr. Kendall, he's the reporter, thinks you did." After a pause, while he closely watched her unexpressive face, he continued, "He thinks you were tried for it." Her hand moved from one of Dog's ears to the other. Her eyes did not open; her face revealed nothing.

Eventually Timmy spoke again. "I'm sorry I brought trouble to you, but I didn't know. I just wanted to help."

Suddenly her claw-like hand reached out and gripped his hand. Her eyes didn't open, she said nothing. Timmy wondered if she could ride a bicycle. "How do you feel?" he asked. She did not answer. Her hand went back to Dog's head.

"If you felt well enough to ride, maybe I could bring my bike down and help you out to it and you wouldn't have to stay here." The face did not change, but the hand did. It stopped stroking Dog's head. "I bet I could bring some of my mother's clothes and they might fit you. She's tall and thin like you—not so thin," he added looking at her appraisingly. "And I have a little money—not much. Maybe you could go back home."

He was surprised to see her eyelids had lifted and she was looking at him.

The Hermit

"You want to do that?" Her eyelids fluttered and he interpreted that as a yes. "Not tomorrow—I'd have to get the clothes and my money is in the bank. It's not much, about $50 but that could help you. Do you think you could manage on your own?" Again the eyelids fluttered.

"I'll take some food up to your house and leave Dog there." He looked at Dog and said apologetically, "I'd have to tie you up, Dog, or you might follow me home. You practice walking—can you?" The eyelids fluttered again, the eyes dark and shining.

"It'll take awhile. Maybe a couple of more weeks. "I'll tell them I'm taking you outside, so you'll need a coat. Are you sure you can ride a bike? There's a big hill." There was a slight nod of the head. Timmy grinned at her. "Okay, I'll do it."

Going home with Dog, doubts assailed him. Certainly it was dumb to think she could ride a bike. He wondered if he shouldn't get his father to help him. No, his father probably wouldn't. Maybe Bob Kendall would help him. No, he couldn't let him in on the secret. And then he thought of Brian's older brother. He had a car. He bet he could get him to do it. How could he manage that? His pedalling slowed. Why would he help him? For money—but if he paid him, he couldn't give much to the Old Lady. He didn't think he would do it just as a favor. The brother and Brian didn't get along too well. Maybe he could make it a dare. Yeah, that might work. He could say that he'd asked Brian if his brother would dare to help someone out of the hospital. Brian said his brother would take any dare.

Timmy felt that was settled, but he'd have to take some things up to the Old Lady's house—it would take a couple of trips, though he could use his school backpack. He could take some food stuff from home—she probably wouldn't be able to forage right away. Maybe he'd better take her someplace else. Wouldn't Kendall immediately think of her old house? He didn't want Kendall to know where she was. Where could he take her? Wait a minute—there was the abandoned schoolhouse. He would take her there!

Chapter Twenty

Timmy started gathering supplies; blankets (2), canned goods and a can opener, bottles of water (he was proud he'd thought of those), and stored them in a large garbage bag in the garage. Having gone down to the cellar one day, he saw a small charcoal burner and he added that. She'd have to gather wood to cook with and that reminded him of matches.

He rode out to the abandoned school and tried the doors. They were locked, of course. He sauntered around the building, looking it over for a place to get in.

She couldn't climb through a window he realized. But if he could get in he could open the door for her. He saw a back door and tried it, not very hopefully. It was locked as he expected. He picked up a fair sized rock and hit the glass panel. The glass shattered with a loud noise. He froze but nobody came charging at him. He hoped it wasn't wired to the police station but he was too impatient to wait and see. He reached in his hand and felt for the door knob. His fingers found the lock knob on the door knob and turned it. He turned the outside knob and he was in! It was creepy and dark.

Leaving the door open, he walked down the hall, opening the doors. As his eyes adjusted to the gloom, he hurried back and closed the outside door. In some of the rooms there was furniture—a desk here, a chair there. More than she had had in her old house. In the restrooms he tried the faucets, but the water had been turned off. And there wouldn't be any heat, but it was already getting warmer outside and this building was lots more solid than her house. She wouldn't be free to sit outside as she had at her old house but she still might be able to sit in the sun in the back.

This would definitely do. He was pleased. In the cafeteria he found pans, even dishes and silverware. Of course the stoves were useless, the gas being turned off. But he was doing her a big favor. This was lots better than her house on the hill.

He biked home, proud of himself. Now he would have to arrange to have Brian's brother bring her out. That would not be easy. He skipped over that and thought about getting her out of the hospital. If he picked a warm day, he'd ask for a wheel chair to take her outside. He didn't remember seeing anybody outside, but there probably would be as the weather got warmer. And he'd bring Dog over before he got her out. Maybe she shouldn't have Dog. Would people notice the big bull mastiff suddenly appearing? But that was what was important to her. He thought of something else to bring—a sleeping bag. It would take several trips to get all that stuff over here. Could he do it all on his bike?

Home, he started taking things from the garbage bag and putting them in the small plastic bags his mother got groceries in. He wondered how he would carry the blankets. He could roll them up and put them on his shoulders, but people would notice. His mother certainly would. Pretend he was sleeping over at his friends'? No, he could do it the days his mother worked and old Mrs. Richards wouldn't notice. He could manage it.

Chapter Twenty One

Timmy made a lot of trips on his bike carry-
ing over the supplies he deemed necessary.
Dog howled when he was left tied up.

Finally he took Dog and rode down to the
nursing home to get in touch with his friend.
(He never thought of her as Cynthia Gray, or
anything else but The Lady.) He and Dog went
to her room but she wasn't there; he put on
her bed the package of clothes he'd brought
for her. He rather liked the red sweater he'd
found in the discard pile his mother kept for
donating to the local thrift shop. It was
pretty. The old lady would like it. He went
to the solarium, but she wasn't there.
Finally he was reduced to asking the nurse
where she was.

"She's been wandering over the whole place.
She's going to be released Friday."

"Released? Where she's going?"

The nurse shrugged her shoulders and
returned to her paper work. "Have no idea."

This changed everything. "When does she get
out?" Timmy asked.

"Eleven's the standard time. The doctor has to see her first."

Timmy groped to his bike outside.

Could she go back to her own dilapidated house? Would Kendall follow her? Wouldn't it be better to take her to the school house where he had everything ready for her and she'd be safe from Kendall?

"I don't know what to do, Dog."

He rode home miserable. Here he'd worked it out so carefully and now there was no point. He could ask his father after all. Would he take her back to her old house? He'd ask him that night.

When his father was settled after dinner in his chair with the paper, Timmy sidled up to the man. "The old lady's going to be released from the nursing home."

"That's nice," his father said not even listening.

"Where do you think she'll go?"

"Home, I s'pose." His father turned pages, folded back the paper and settled down to the editorial page.

"Would you take her there?"

"Um," his father muttered.

"She can't walk that far, Dad," Timmy persisted.

Timmy's urgency finally penetrated his father's attention. He lowered the paper and glared at the boy. "What're you talking about?"

"The old lady."

"That again? It's not our business." He returned to the paper.

"Don't we have to help people if we can?"

His father glared at him from around the

The Hermit

paper. "And what do you think our obligation is?"

Timmy winced at the growl but remained staunch. "I guess I got her into this. I interfered." His voice was apologetic.

"And now?"

Timmy hesitated and then asked, "What do you think I should do?"

"She isn't your concern. If you want to, call the Salvation Army and have them take over." The newspaper was raised and he settled back.

Timmy wandered away. Should he call the Salvation Army? He couldn't do that. She'd hate it. Maybe he could go back to his original plan and have Brian's brother drive her to the school. It was the only sensible solution.

He would do that tomorrow.

Chapter Twenty Two

───────

It was after breakfast and Tim headed out to Brian's. Brian was out in his swing when Timmy entered his yard. "Hi, Brian, where's your brother?"

"Who'd want to know where Kevin is?" Brian sneered.

"You have a fight with him?" Tim asked.

"He's a jerk."

Timothy decided this was not an appropriate time to ask a favor. "I hear that about older brothers." There was no sound but the slight creaking of the slowly moving swing. "What happened?"

"Wouldn't take me when he went off this morning."

Timothy felt relief; he wouldn't have to tackle the brother this morning. But time was his enemy. Friday was tomorrow. He had to get the plan set up. "Where'd he go?"

"He wouldn't tell me." Brian stubbed his toe into the ground, making the swing circle. "Bet he went racing."

"Racing? He races with his car?"

"Think so. Chicken racing."

"He races chickens?"

Brian laughed. "Naw. Other kids—you're a chicken if you don't take risks to win. It's 'citing."

"Why wouldn't he take you?"

"'Fraid I'd tell."

"Would you?"

"Naw."

"Have you ever gone racing with him?"

"Once, but he didn't know."

"You hid?"

"Yeah, I was in the back of the car. It scared me, but it was sort of fun, too."

"I need your brother," Timmy said suddenly.

Brian was startled. "Why on earth?"

"I need him to drive my friend. Do you think he would?"

"Who's the friend?" There was a little resentment in his tone.

"She's an old lady. My Dad won't help her, but I've got to help her." Timmy turned and scraped a circle in the dirt at his feet. "Do you think your brother would help?"

"Naw, why would he?"

"Well," Timothy moved uncomfortably, "I thought maybe if you just asked him." He spoke with difficulty, "If he was afraid you'd tell on him. Did he ever find out you'd been with him racing that time?"

Brian stared at him. "Threaten him?"

"Yeah, I guess."

Brian stared at him and then grinned. "I think it might work. Sorta fun, huh?"

Timothy grinned in response. "Give me a call tonight if it works."

Chapter Twenty Three

Tim got his cell Thursday night.

Brian and Kevin waited for him at Brian's corner. Kevin was sulky but willing to drive. He drove to the nursing home and parked near the entrance. Timmy got out by himself and ran to the old lady's room. She was dressed in clothes and wore the red sweater Timmy had brought. Her own clothes had been discarded. She nodded to Timmy, but did not speak

"Have you been seen by the doctor? Have you been dismissed?"

She nodded.

"Good. Come with me. I can take you home."

He reached out for her hand and she allowed him to lead her out. He noticed that she walked fairly well, one foot was a little draggy but she was only slightly stooped. They went to the elevator. A nurse looked up as they passed the main desk.

"Where are you going, Jane?"

"My father is waiting downstairs," Timmy said quickly.

The nurse rose. "You have to be in a wheel

chair," she addressed the old lady. "Are you taking her to your house?" she asked as she rolled over a wheel chair.

"No. She's going out to her own home."

The nurse shuffled through a file. "It says here that where she came from was inadequate."

"We fixed it up," Timmy promptly supplied and pushed the Old Lady into the elevator.

There, she spoke. "Home?"

"Not quite. A new place," Timmy said quickly.

When they went out of the building, an alert Brian waved at them and Kevin drove over. Timmy helped her into the back of the car and pushed the wheel chair back to the entrance.

"Bags?" Kevin asked.

"None," Timmy said jumping in. "Go to the corner of Sycamore and Comet," he directed.

He saw Kevin looking at him curiously, but he asked nothing more. Timmy worried that too many people knew where she would be, but he'd had to have help.

"Home?" she muttered inquiringly.

"Not really." Timmy turned to her. "A different place—closer to me so I can help you."

She turned puzzled eyes on him. "Want home," she protested.

"Just for awhile," he soothed.

"Dog?"

"I'll bring him later. I couldn't do it this morning." They got to their destination and Kevin stopped. "Here? This is the old school they closed."

"Drive around back," Timmy ordered. Kevin reluctantly drove to the parking lot back of the school. It's cement was breaking up, but it was driveable.

"What's going on?"

"It's okay. Thanks. You can go now." Timmy helped the old Lady out of the car and waved goodbye, but Kevin did not leave. "This sure smells funny. It doesn't make sense."

Timmy said, "Brian and I won't tell about the chicken racing," and waved dismissively. Kevin stared at him and then shrugged, and drove off.

Timmy led the Old Lady to the door and opened it and urged her in. She moved unwillingly, looking around. Timmy led her to the room he had prepared, the sleeping bag and the two blankets, a couple of old folding canvas chairs he'd brought over and boxes of supplies. He led her to a chair and gently half pushed her into it. "See—better than your other place. There's a charcoal burner—it's small but it will do. And food—see here in these boxes. Eggs and bread and dry milk and a couple of jugs of water. I tried to think of everything." He turned proudly to her.

"Dog," she mourned and then she stood up. "Home."

"I'm afraid to take you to your real home. I was afraid that reporter would find you. He's trying to prove you're Cynthia Gray. You'll be safe from him here."

Timmy picked out of another box, "And here's a flashlight." He took it over to her and put it in her hand and pushed her fingers down so that it lit. "See, you'll have a little light. Not much."

She looked at him sadly and said softly, "Home."

"Maybe later, when you're really well again. I'm going home now, and I'll bring Dog back after lunch. He'll stay here with you. Don't go out in front but there's a wood in back. No one will see you there."

She stood there looking sad. He led her over to the window. "See, woods. Don't you think Dog will like that?"

"Home," she announced firmly.

"This is your home for a little while. Maybe a month," Timmy said.

He went back into the corridor but she did not follow. He left the building. Since he couldn't lock the door, he stood at the corner of the building awhile to see if she would follow him out. She did not.

I thought she'd like it, he mused. It's better than where she was living. He hurried the several blocks to his home.

Chapter Twenty Four

When Tim returned with Dog he opened the door.
Dog, tail wagging, entered. They went down to
the room Timmy had selected. It was empty.

"Lady," Tim called. "Lady, where are you?"
He turned to the dog, "Dog, find her." But
Dog just stood there, waiting.

Slowly, Tim went through all the rooms.
They were as empty as they had been when he
first broke in.

"She left," he said to Dog. "And I thought
she'd like it. Where do you suppose she went?
She couldn't find her old home."

That gave him an idea. "Maybe she went into
the woods." He raced to the door and they
plunged outside, dashing to the woods. "Find
her, Dog."

But Dog lazily investigated clumps of grass
and trees. Timmy tried to remember how to
track and he looked on the ground to see if
there were footprints. He could find none. He
and Dog wandered into the woods and Timmy
found paths and followed them, but he did not
discover his friend.

Elizabeth H. Noble

At last he dismally returned to his bike at the school door. He snapped the leash onto Dog. "I don't know what I can do now."

What he could do was ride home, which he did. He went in the house and his mother promptly said, "There you are. The school called and wanted to know why you weren't there."

"Wha'd you tell them?"

"I said I didn't know. What did you think I would tell them? Where have you been?"

"My friend got out of the hospital." And suddenly tears were dripping down his face. "I took her where she'd be safe and now she's gone!"

His mother came and kneeling beside him, cuddled him in her arms. "What friend?"

"The Old Lady! You know!"

Slowly she released him. "I thought we were through with her. She was released from the hospital and you don't know where she is?"

Timmy shook her head. "I took her to a place I'd fixed up for her. Can't you understand?"

"How could you take her? No, I don't understand."

Timmy darted away from her, but she grabbed his arm and held him. "What do you mean you took her?"

"From the hospital!"

"On foot?"

"No." Timmy scraped at his dripping nose. "A friend drove her."

"What friend?"

"I don't know—just a friend."

"You just asked someone driving by to pick up this patient from the hospital?"

The Hermit

"Something like that."

"I don't believe you." She stood up. "Suppose you tell me the truth, Timmy."

"I have," he blurted, "mostly. I can't tell who helped—he'd get in trouble. But anyway, he drove us—to where I'd fixed up."

"Fixed up? Is that where my blankets disappeared to? And where is this?"

Timmy shuffled, "Some of your clothes, too."

This she let drop, merely asking gently, "And where was this place?"

"Sycamore and Comet."

"Somebody's house?"

Timmy shook his head but said nothing. His mother thought but then realization came. "The abandoned school—You broke into that school?"

Timmy nodded.

"Timothy! That's terrible."

He raised tear filled eyes. "She's gone. She left. I don't know where she is." His chin quivered.

"I think this is something your father's going to have to deal with. Timmy, didn't it occur to you that it was against the law to break into that school?"

"But she needed a place to stay. Bob would find her if I took her back to her home!"

"Who's Bob?"

"That reporter."

"Oh, yes, I remember. Why would he want to find her?"

Timmy broke down again. "He thinks she murdered somebody.

He's trying to prove it. And now I've lost her." He turned urgently to his mother. "She won't be able to find her way back to her home. She's all alone and lost."

His mother again put her arms around him as he sobbed. Finally she said, "We could tell the police that this old, confused woman left the hospital and apparently is wandering around. They can look for her and take care of her."

Chapter Twenty Five

Kendall was just finishing his coffee when his doorbell rang. Still clutching his napkin he answered and stared down at a weeping boy. "Timmy, what are you doing here? How'd you know where I live?"

The boy blurted out, "She's gone. She's lost and it's all my fault."

Kendall stepped back and motioned the boy in. "Your old lady?"

Timmy nodded and said tearfully, "I thought she'd stay. But when I took Dog back, she was gone."

"C'mon in and tell me from the beginning. First, how'd you find me?"

"Mom said maybe you could help—with the paper and all. Let people know she was wandering around and not dangerous or nuts or something. And she said we could find you in the telephone book, and we did. Can you help?"

"How'd you get her from the nursing home?"

Timmy poured out the story in a rush of words, ending, "I wanted to help her. I thought I was!"

"I know you were helping her, Timmy," the man said gently, "and now she's wandering around town, is that right?"

Timmy nodded forlornly.

"Well, she doesn't get around very well, does she."

"She can walk. They said she was wandering all over the hospital—I'd told her to practice walking." Timmy looked down and added almost inaudibly, "I was going to sneak her out of the hospital, but they released her before I could."

"Well, let's get into my car and take a look around. Your mother knows you're here?"

Timmy nodded as he snuffled the remaining tears away.

The two of them went out the back door to the garage. Suddenly Timmy yelped, "In the garbage pail, it's her!" Bob glanced up, caught a glimpse of a red sweater and Timmy dashing over the lawn to the neighbor's.

"Lady, lady, I've found you!"

The old woman, who had tried to run, was stopped as the boy came charging toward her and put his arms around her.

She stood there dumb, her arms flailing uncertainly.

Bob Kendall strode over. "He was pretty upset to find you gone. Do you want to go to your house on the hill?"

Her eyes glistened as she said, "Home?"

"Do you want me to take you home?" the reporter asked again.

She nodded, saying, "Home, home."

He turned to the boy and gently put his hand on the boy's arm. "Is that okay, Timmy. She just wants to go back to her house."

The Hermit

Timmy nodded, clutching her boney hand tightly.

"You had things for her. Shall we go pick some things up?" Timmy nodded. Between the two of them they led her to Kendall's car, strapped her in and locked the door.

"It was that abandoned school, wasn't it, Timmy? Right on our way."

"Thanks," Timmy said, nodding in agreement. When they drove in around the back of the school, the Old Lady started protesting, fighting against the straps. "Home, home" she demanded.

"It's all right, we're taking you there. Run in, Timmy and get some blankets, food and clothes. But hurry, she's getting very upset."

Timmy ran, sweeping up the sleeping bag and blankets and a few clothes and running back to the car. Kendall stored them in the trunk and hurriedly started the car.

"It's all right," Timmy said, turning around in the front seat and holding out his hand to her. "We're taking you up to your home. I'll bring Dog up tomorrow. You'll want Dog, won't you."

It did not take long to get up the hills and slowly go down the road, both Timmy and Bob watching for the faint trace of the path.

Suddenly the old lady exclaimed and struggled with the door. Kendall stopped the car and Timmy jumped out to release her. Kendall unlocked the door and she got out, starting down the overgrown path, Timmy followimg. She limped painfully forward, eager.

Kendall brought out the things rescued from the school and trailed behind the other two.

When they arrived at the decrepit house, she burst in. Timmy, a moment behind her, saw her hands clasped and she was murmuring, "Home. Home."

"She wants it," he said, glancing at his friend.

"Not my idea of 'Home Sweet Home,'" the reporter muttered, dropping his burden. "Are you sure you want to stay?" he asked.

She paid no attention to him but moved out to the porch. Bob and Timmy left, walking back to his car.

"I was so afraid she was lost," Timmy said as he got in the car again. "I'll bring Dog out to her tomorrow, and maybe some food. You do think she'll be all right, don't you?"

"It's what she wants. It wouldn't be what I want, but all we can do is what she wants. That ramshackled building is home to her. She's glad to be there."

Timmy looked at him sharply. "Are you still trying to prove she's Cynthia Gray? That she killed that guy?"

Bob Kendall was silent for a while as he drove, thinking over the question. He glanced down at the intense face beside him. "Can't see what point there is, do you?" Then regretfully, "Would have made a good story though."

Timmy's face lit with his relief. "Oh, gee, thanks." Then after reflecting a moment, he added, "What I'd fixed for her was lots better'n than that old house." His voice was sad about the lack of appreciation but then he added, "She'll be glad to see Dog." His voice showed his contentment.